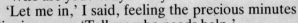

I pulled out the gold
front of their eyes. It

'*Gott in Himmel!*' s
sake!'

She broke off and s

'Who are you? Why

'Let me in,' I said, feeling the precious minutes
slipping away. 'Tell me who needs help.'

The man seemed to want to silence her, and
began to push her back, but the woman drew in her
breath sharply and answered me with sudden
urgency.

'It's the Baroness Adèle—but you're——' She
stopped again, and looked quickly behind her.
'She's coming—that woman—you must go!'

'*Tell me!*' I said insistently.

'There's no time! Come tomorrow—go *now*—
go!'

Evelyn Stewart Armstrong was educated in Bath. In 1941 she joined the *BBC Engineering Division* and worked at Bush House, London on technical control of the European Services, handling news broadcasts and code messages. In 1946 she went to British European Airways as an air stewardess and flew until 1951, when she married Charles Armstrong, a customs officer.

They moved to a village above the Romney Marsh, where Evelyn began to write novels. Five years ago they retired to the south of Spain, where they bought and renovated an old Andalusian farmhouse. She now does her writing at a window overlooking cork woods and the peaks of the Sierra Blanquilla. *The Keepsake* is her second Masquerade Historical Romance.

THE KEEPSAKE

Evelyn Stewart Armstrong

MILLS & BOON LIMITED
15–16 BROOK'S MEWS
LONDON W1A 1DR

*First published in Great Britain 1986
by Mills & Boon Limited*

© Evelyn Stewart Armstrong 1983

*Australian copyright 1986
Philippine copyright 1986
This edition 1986*

ISBN 0 263 75480 4

Set in 11 on 11½ pt Linotron Times
04–0986–66,800

*Photoset by Rowland Phototypesetting Limited
Bury St Edmunds, Suffolk
Made and printed in Great Britain by
Cox & Wyman Limited, Reading*

CHAPTER ONE

I WAS STANDING on the platform of the Gare de l'Est in Paris. Beside me loomed and stretched, carriage after carriage, the great shining snake, all gleaming paint and glittering metal, which was the Orient Express.

The quality of the voices all around me, their pitch and intonation, the whiffs of coffee and garlic and French tobacco would have told me had I been blindfolded that I was in France; and the sounds and smells were complemented, amplified by everything I saw. Every inch of the train shone in the splendid electric lights of the station, and along each car the words '*Compagnie Internationale des Wagons-Lits et des Grands Express Européens*' were proudly blazoned; this was the most modern, the quickest, the most luxurious way to travel.

The platform was crowded with people: humble porters and sweepers in heavy boots and blue smocks were sprinkled here and there among the passengers, of whom there was an infinite variety. Then there were the train attendants, all in spruce uniforms, but with subtle differences showing their rank and function. Many, of course, were inside the cars, but a number of conductors were helping the passengers, and the imposing figure to whom they deferred was plainly the *chef de train*. The passengers, diverse as they were, had one thing in common— wealth. It was as well, I thought, that I was amply provided for; I should otherwise have been at a disadvantage among so many people born to luxury or having acquired the means of rising to it. The toilettes of the ladies and the clothes of the gentlemen, though not always in good taste, were invariably expensive; an array of broadcloth with silk facings; tall hats and gold watchchains; a parade of folds and flounces in rich materials embellished with braid, sparked with diamonds and topped with little hats covered in veiling and feathers.

For the time being I forgot that I had the most serious, the saddest of reasons for my journey, and enjoyed myself quizzing my possible travelling companions. A lady was mounting the car quite close to me; her black grosgrain gown billowed out from underneath a matching cape which fell back to reveal a lining of deep violet, and there were bunches of violets on her hat. She was, I supposed, in her late thirties, and in her way a beauty, but I found her face hard, her expression calculating, which to me diminished her charm. I thought, too, that she was wearing too many jewels for a train journey—what would she wear to the Opera?

She disappeared, and further down the platform two magnificent figures came strolling along. They were officers in uniform, and I guessed them to be Hungarians, for surely no other European army would wear anything so splendidly exotic? One of them had buff breeches and a green tunic frogged with gold, over which was slung a great wolf-skin. The other had white breeches and a tunic of sky-blue, with a dolman jacket of darker blue bearing even more gold braid than his companion.

A gentleman passed by me, and for a moment our glances met. He was English, unmistakably so, and I had the impression that I had seen him before. Indeed he looked as if he were ready to give me a bow of acknowledgment, but my lack of obvious recognition stopped him. He was dressed with quiet excellence in frock-coat and silk hat, with a Chesterfield overcoat on his arm, though I hardly noticed his clothes until later, for the thing that stirred my memory was the contrast between his dark skin and his clear grey eyes. His features were good: a straight nose, a strong, well-shaped mouth; but the piercing quality of those eyes made me think I had seen him once before, if only in passing. He, too, went up into the car.

My companion, Lady Bellanger—small, grey-haired, with a quietly commanding manner—was glancing imperiously about her, having to wait a full five seconds while a uniformed attendant approached us, ready to check our reservations and usher us to our places. Unlike me, nothing else concerned her. If she was aware of anything, I have no doubt it was that she was out of England and therefore nothing would be up to English standards. Except, of course, the Orient Express—that was why she had chosen it, and the Express, after all, was international.

Now our tickets were checked; with a great deal of bustling and the deferential help of the conductor Lady Bellanger entered the carriage. I followed, and Stevens, Lady Bellanger's maid, mounted after us. Almost at once, and before reaching our compartment, Lady Bellanger came face to face with the grey-eyed man.

'Why, Captain Talbot! I did not know you were travelling today!'

'It is my pleasure to find you on the train, Lady Bellanger.'

She turned to me.

'Charlotte, I do not think you have met Captain Talbot? Captain, this is Lady Charlotte Brantham. We have joined forces for the journey.'

He bowed over my hand, and it was a mark in his favour that he did not murmur some inanity such as 'a double delight' which was the usual way of men in society. And at that moment Lady Bellanger's calling him *Captain* Talbot reminded me where I had seen him before, and why I had not recognised him. We had met in a room of the Foreign Office in London, and he had then been in uniform.

It was from the Foreign Office that I had received news of my father's death. The shock had been very great, and I had had no preparation for it; when we had said our goodbyes he had been in the best of health. I was told he had contracted typhoid fever and had died in a little village some miles from Vienna. He had been among strangers; not even his servant had been with him. When my father had decided to go to Vienna, Blake had been ill with influenza, and Papa had settled to travel alone and engage a temporary man on arrival. If his stay should be prolonged, Blake could follow when fit. Blake arrived too late; my father was dead and buried. I was given the news the day after Blake's departure; he returned with nothing but the few effects with which my father had travelled.

When I opened the cases, I saw they were packed with Blake's impeccable neatness; there were

Papa's clothes, his toilet articles, and in a little packet his most personal things—his pocket-book, with English and foreign money in it, a notebook, a gold pencil, my photograph, his gold watch and chain—and the keepsake.

This last had hung on his watchchain with his seal-fob for as long as I could remember. I suppose, being used to seeing it there from babyhood, I paid it no particular attention, regarding it and his fob as something shining and dangling with which to play when he took me on his knee. I must have been about nine or ten when I first had the impulse to look at it closely. The fob I had seen in use countless times when my father sealed his letters, but the oval gold medallion had no apparent function, it was simply an ornament. My little fingers took it and turned it from one side to the other; one face had a coat of arms upon it which was not that of our family, the other bore one word in strange writing, and the word was unintelligible to me.

'What is this, Papa?' I asked, my curiosity at last aroused.

'A foreign token, my dear,' he answered.

'A token? Why is it always on your watchchain?'

'Because it was a keepsake.'

'What is the picture on it? It looks like a bird with flames around it.'

'It is a mythical bird called a phoenix.'

'Where did it come from?'

'From Vienna. Now, Charlie, are you going to show me how well you can read today?'

Because I always loved to win his approval, this easily sidetracked me, and I soon realised with a child's sensitivity that the keepsake was not to be discussed.

I was an only child, leading a happy, uneventful life. I adored my parents, and between them there existed a serene affection which bound us all together as a contented, united family. My father was not an idle aristocrat. He combined great intelligence with considerable charm, and his knowledge of international affairs and diplomacy was often used in a completely unofficial manner by the government. He often travelled abroad, being absent for several weeks at a time, and when he returned laden with presents for Mama and me, he would entertain us with descriptions of balls and dinners, drives and parties which I realised later were the trivia; serious matters which might have been the real reason for his travels were never mentioned.

While he was abroad, I stayed at home with Mama, for she never went with him; she was, she said, a poor traveller. Perhaps this was an excuse, but my trust in my parents was so complete that I accepted it without question. Then, when I was fifteen and looking forward to being launched in society, my mother died. I was desolate and inconsolable; I clung to my father and begged him never to leave me.

After a period of mourning and a further decent interval, I was 'brought out' by one of my father's sisters. It was a quiet début, for we were not in the mood for parties, but I did not wish to remain officially a child for longer than was necessary. I had my plans: I intended to travel with Papa. And, after considerable persuasion, he agreed, even though it meant he had the trouble of arranging a chaperon for me wherever we went. There was always some friendly matron in the British Embassy or Legation who was willing to oblige us, and take me round with her when my father was occupied. So, during two varied years, I had stayed in France, Germany, Sweden, Portugal and Italy —but not Austria. Thinking back as far as I could remember, I could not recall my father ever having gone to Austria, and Vienna was never mentioned except in geography lessons as the capital of the Austro-Hungarian Empire, and, just once, as the origin of the keepsake.

Savagely I said to myself as I looked through his travelling bags, If he had never gone there, he would have been alive today.

I remembered very clearly the arrival of the letter—if you could call it that. Papa and I were sitting at the breakfast table when the footman brought in the morning mail. He took the letters from the salver and glanced through them to see if any were for me. One bore a foreign stamp, and I noticed that for a moment he paused, sitting quite still, holding it and looking at it, all expression wiped from his face. Without saying a word he put down the other letters, picked up the paper-knife which had lain across the pile, and slit the envelope. It was empty. I saw him put his fingers in to take out the folded paper, and encounter nothing. Then he turned the envelope upside down, and something fluttered out on the tablecloth and from there fell to the floor. It landed by my foot, and before Papa could do so, I stooped and picked it up. It was a piece of paper roughly torn off, it seemed, from the top of a sheet of writing-paper bearing a crest; underneath was scrawled one word, nothing else. The writing was in a foreign hand, the word was in German, 'Help,' and the crest was the same as that on my father's keepsake.

I said nothing, but handed it to him. I looked at him, then looked away, for I could not bear that frozen stillness which had descended on him, making his face like a mask, himself an automaton whose hand moved, whose fingers took the paper, totally unaware of his surroundings or even of my existence. I stared down at the envelope in his other hand; it had been addressed to him care of the Foreign Office, and forwarded. I wondered why he should receive a call for help from someone who wrote like a child or a near-illiterate. Such writing and an aristocratic crest seemed quite incompatible. We both sat there, frozen, like two characters out of the Sleeping Beauty, for what could have been no more than a few seconds but seemed an age. Then my father put the paper in the envelope, and sorted through the rest of the letters.

'Only one for you, Charlie.'

His voice sounded almost normal, and he began opening his other letters as if nothing unusual had happened. I asked no questions then. I was not afraid of my father. He would not have frowned sternly and said, 'Do not be impertinent, miss. It is none of your business', as so many fathers might have done. But I guessed he had had a shock; the matter was somehow painful, and I must bide my time.

After breakfast he went to his study and stayed there behind closed doors for about half an hour.

When he came out, he had the air of a man who had made a decision, and I knew that my time had come.

'I must go abroad, Charlie, as soon as I can make arrangements to travel.'

'To Austria, Papa?'

'Yes, my dear.'

'I can be ready as soon as you are.'

'This time, Charlotte, you cannot come with me.'

'But, Papa, couldn't I help?'

'No. This is a hurried business, and I can make no plans. You must stay and keep house for me here.'

Keep house! It had never been necessary before. I felt I was being fobbed off like a twelve-year-old. I bit my lip and said nothing. He put his arm round me.

'Charlie—it's not that I don't want you. It's just not possible for you to come. I don't know what is ahead of me.'

What was ahead of him, as it turned out, was death.

I received two letters from him—two totally non-committal letters. I felt betrayed. I never expected to be told about his semi-official business, that was not for me, yet I had travelled with him and so remained part of his life. But this—this was different. The matter was personal, I was sure of that, and yet he had not confided in me; I had been deliberately excluded, and I did not know why. Someone had appealed to him for help, and he had given me no explanation. He had said nothing at the time, nor did he mention it in his letters. 'Vienna is a fine city, the countryside is beautiful, in the vineyards they are selling the new wine . . .' and so on.

When I had recovered from the initial shock of his death, I realised I would not rest until I had the answer to one question. It was pointless to ask myself why he had died; what was gnawing at my brain and would not give me peace was the need to know why he had gone to the place where death had met him.

To go to Vienna was not as easy for me as you might expect. I could not simply say to my maid, 'Pack a bag', and to the butler, 'Get me tickets to Vienna'. For one thing, I could not travel alone —even with a maid I should have invited all sorts of unwelcome attentions and encounters, and tongues would have wagged so that I would have returned with a reputation in tatters. The family name meant enough to me not to risk that. In the past some of the Branthams have said that we were once connected with the French line of Brantôme, but that means nothing to me. To be the daughter of Hilary Brantham is enough, and no one was going to have the opportunity of saying I had behaved like a slut, trailing my petticoats all the way to Vienna and back. So I had to have a chaperon, and for that I needed a reason for going. The one reason I could not give was the real one—no English matron would have countenanced my going abroad to try to ferret out a private mystery to which I had no clue other than the coat of arms on a gold medallion.

But I soon thought of a reason that would be perfectly convincing and acceptable. What devoted daughter would not wish to visit her father's grave?

An official from the Foreign Office had called on me to break the news of my father's death, and so it was to that department I applied, saying that I wished to see the place where he was buried, and asking whether they could suggest a suitable chaperon. I must mention that my aunts, all five of them on both sides of the family, were too old, infirm, occupied with family cares or in some other way unable to travel with me. I was not sorry; they would have asked too many questions.

I received a reply to my letter which was courteous though brief, requesting my attendance at a certain date and time to meet my proposed chaperon. I went to the Foreign Office, presented my letter, and was shown into an anteroom. I had been there only a minute when an inner door was opened—but whoever should have come out was called back. The door was left not quite shut; there was a murmur of voices, and then one was raised more loudly. I distinctly heard the words, 'I do not consider it part of my duties, sir, to dance attendance on a little chit who is indulging in maudlin sentimentality.'

There was a quiet response, another word or two, and then the door opened, properly this time, and a man in cavalry uniform came out, his dark face unsmiling, his mouth set, an angry frown pulling down the brows over his dark-lashed, pale grey eyes. He marched past me with a clink of spurs, giving me one long stare as he went. That was my first sight of Captain Piers Talbot.

I thought to myself, What a bad-tempered man! I am sorry for the girl he is going to be obliged to escort. Then I was called for my interview, and at once forgot him.

On our second meeting he looked more agreeable; his detested escort duties were over, I supposed. He even asked Lady Bellanger whether he might join us for dinner, and she readily agreed.

'So nice to have a protective male,' she said to me.

I know it is only in the past few years that women have been able to travel alone on the railways —and then they frequently arm themselves with hat-pins—but I felt that in 1888 on the Orient Express it was hardly likely that a dowager such as Lady Bellanger would be subject to any attack or even to the mildest of verbal offence. On the Orient Express, I thought, one would be safer than anywhere.

No lady need suffer the presence of a man for a moment longer than she chose. First, her compartment was totally private. Every sleeping-car had two single and three double compartments—Lady Bellanger and I were sharing a double, as we had made late bookings and all the singles had been taken. The compartment was beautifully furnished, with panelling of inlaid woods and soft upholstered seats, which the attendant later converted into two beds, made up with sheets and blankets and eiderdown of the finest quality. There were blinds and curtains which could be drawn closely over the windows, and a bell to summon the attendant, and a speaking-tube direct to the conductor who sat at the end of the car.

But one was not obliged to stay in one's compartment; further along the train was a ladies' drawing-room with little gilded upholstered chairs and sofas and Watteau-like tapestries on the walls—a French boudoir into which no man would dare set foot. For the gentlemen, Lady Bellanger told me, there was a smoking-room with books, newspapers and maps, and deep leather armchairs like a London club.

We settled ourselves in our compartment, and I had hardly finished admiring its furnishings when I heard the cry, *'En voiture, messieurs, s'il vous plaît!'* The snap of closing doors rattled along the train, followed by whistles and hisses, an almost imperceptible jerk as the powerful engine took the strain, and then, slowly at first, majestically, and steadily gathering speed, we steamed out of the station. I looked at my watch. It was exactly seven-thirty. The Orient Express was never late.

We had left London in the morning of a dull November day, raw and misty, and were swaddled up in thick cloaks; Lady Bellanger said that in Vienna it would be much colder. The channel crossing had been rough, and the journey from Calais to Paris tedious, but now we could make ourselves really comfortable. Our first act was to shed our cloaks, for the compartment had a heating system and was delightfully warm. Tomorrow evening, I told myself, I shall be in Vienna. It seemed incredible that the journey took less than twenty-eight hours.

We watched what little we could from our window—not much more than a few glimmering lights here and there—we chatted, we read a little, and quite soon, it seemed, the attendant tapped gently on our door and announced that dinner would be served in fifteen minutes.

'It was most agreeable of Captain Talbot to offer us his company, even if he has no acquaintance on the train,' Lady Bellanger remarked. 'But there, he is a perfect gentleman.'

About his breeding she knew more than I did, but as for acquaintances, I noticed that as the two Hungarian officers passed the three of us at table, they exchanged nods with him.

We had seen the officers in the corridor; the one in green made way for me rather ostentatiously, giving me a long gaze which was probably intended to be admiring. It did not register well with me, for his lean face and glittering eyes had a wolfish look, appropriate, I thought, to a man who wore a wolf-skin. The other, the one in blue, was fair, with rather effeminate features and a spoilt, ill-tempered set to his mouth.

The dining-car was magnificent, ornate with panelling, carving and gilding. I had never ex-pected such luxury on a train. I was staggered when Captain Talbot told me that the small framed pic-tures between the windows were original paintings by some of the most famous artists of our time —one I admired he told me was by Delacroix! The gas-lit chandeliers with their cut-glass pendants lit up the fine napery and delicate glass, the silver and porcelain; the meal was served by waiters in tail-coats and knee-breeches. The meal itself was superb, the finest French cuisine, at least seven courses—I lost count—but I remember there was caviar, lobster, some most delicious game, and a sorbet of amazing delicacy.

The two Hungarian officers were joined by the lady with the violets—only now she had shed her hat and cloak and was wearing a head-dress of veiling caught up with diamond crescents. Lady Bellanger did not fail to notice this.

'Countess Plesch,' she hissed at Captain Talbot, 'will one day take things too far.'

He smiled, apparently knowing what she was talking about. I could only assume she was referring to the lady's rather ostentatious style of dress.

The Captain was agreeable enough as a table companion, but I could not help noticing that the Hungarian officers' party was much more lively. They laughed and joked together, and from the odd snippets of phrases that I overheard they seemed to be exchanging a great deal of gossip. I understood very little; they were speaking German, in which I was moderately fluent, but it was German much modified by a strange soft accent which I then assumed to be Hungarian but later discovered was Viennese.

At one point when our conversation flagged, curiosity forced me to ask a question of the Captain.

'Please tell me, Captain Talbot—those officers behind you—is not their uniform Hungarian? Yet they seem to be speaking German.'

'They are speaking Austrian,' he corrected me. 'Hungary is part of the Empire, and all officers of their regiments must speak it. All orders are given in Austrian. Most of the officers are bilingual—though I suspect some of them do not speak Hungarian nearly as well as they speak Austrian.'

'How strange,' I remarked.

'Not really,' he retorted drily. 'You would hardly

expect an officer of the Welsh Guards to speak Welsh all the time.'

I began to be irritated by the way that the Captain treated me conversationally as little more than a child. He was, I guessed, nearing thirty; but at eighteen I was, though inexperienced by his standards, not an ignoramus. There came a point when he glossed over something as being beyond my understanding, and I could not contain my annoyance.

'Captain Talbot!' I said sharply. 'I have not the benefit of your years, but I have been educated, and I am not a fool. I understand quite well what you are talking about.'

'My apologies, Lady Charlotte,' he replied smoothly. 'I was not aware that we had a blue-stocking among us.'

To contradict that, after insisting on my knowledge, would make me look like a petulant child, so I said nothing, and he had won. I thought, What an infuriating man! Lady Bellanger might find him attractive, but he has no charm for me. I could never feel sentimentally disposed to someone with grey eyes like gimlets. That was as well, for he was plainly indifferent to me.

He did not even trouble to ask me the reason for my visit to Vienna, and Lady Bellanger did not mention it. In this she may have been more tactful than I gave her credit for. But he had plenty of information about the Express, which I found most interesting. It surprised me that his conversation with us never touched on military subjects; I would never have suspected him of being a soldier. One, or at the most two, dinners with him would be enough, I decided. I was quite glad to think I was unlikely to see anything of the Captain once I reached Vienna.

So, after a pleasant dinner, Lady Bellanger and I went back to our compartment and prepared for bed. At length, lying in comfort, gently rocked by the train with its steady sounds acting as a kind of lullaby, I fell asleep. Would I have slept so well if I had known what lay ahead of me? Most certainly I would not, yet I hope, had I had the knowledge and the choice, I would still have continued with my plan. I was my father's daughter; he was dead, but I wanted no mystery between us.

The Express throbbed through the night, the rhythmic thrumming of the wheels like the beats of a heart. The rhythm only changed, slowed and stopped when the train paused to take on water and fuel. The halts hardly disturbed me. On an average, a mere five minutes were spent on necessary services, and one could doze through the subdued sounds of outside activity. We had stopped at Bar-le-Duc at about twenty minutes before midnight; the other halts I ignored, but when I woke to a dim early light I saw that it was seven in the morning and that we were on the platform of the station at Carlsruhe.

Breakfast was served in our compartment; we were at Stuttgart at twenty minutes past nine. We spent the morning in the ladies' drawing-room, where we saw some of the other female passengers —but not the Countess Plesch. Neither did the other lady in our car appear. I had glimpsed her in the corridor the previous evening, and seen her in the dining-car with her husband, but I caught no sight of her that morning until luncheon. On looking back I find it strange that all the members of our sleeping-car played a part in the events which I was to encounter. We were all so different. In the two single compartments were Captain Talbot and Countess Plesch, the two Hungarian officers shared one double, the married couple had another, and Lady Bellanger and I were in the third.

To me the married couple seemed dull and uninteresting. They were middle-aged Viennese; she was somewhat plump, and very plainly dressed; had her clothes not been of such excellent quality, one would have been tempted to call her dowdy. She was rather colourless, nondescript. Nondescript brown hair, a pale face with nondescript features, a nondescript manner of sitting and listening to her husband, nodding agreement, saying, it seemed, nothing but '*Ja*'.

I noticed them at luncheon, when he was doing all the talking—not that he said a great deal. He was short and broad, with greying hair, a heavy-featured face, with sidewhiskers and a moustache which half-hid a thin-lipped mouth. He was wearing a black frock-coat, a high winged collar and a pale grey cravat with a pearl pin, and a pair of pince-nez was attached by a fine chain to his lapel. He looked like some kind of professional man—a lawyer, perhaps. At all events he seemed to lay down the law to his wife, shooting a few sentences over the table to her, emphasised by a wagging finger, to which she would say, '*Ja*', and then he would return to his meal until the next idea struck him. They were too far down the car for me to have any idea what he was saying: I could see only his wife's dutifully nodding head, and lip-read her '*Ja*'. But they seemed so dull that I thought no more of them, and never expected to see either of them again.

At two thirty-five in the afternoon, we reached Munich. Lady Bellanger told me we were now exactly two hundred and seventy miles from Vienna.

Excitement and a certain nervousness began to make themselves known to me. What was I going to do? I really had no plans. My initial moves had been settled for me. Lady Bellanger was the wife of an official on the staff of the British Ambassador, and having agreed to chaperon me on the journey, had invited me to stay with her. I was glad of such kindness; it was plain I must inflict myself on somebody, and I did not wish to have to ask the British Ambassador for too many favours. It had already been indicated that I would be taken by a member of his staff to the church in the village where my father had died. I hoped I would not find it difficult to prolong my stay until I found out what I had come to discover. I was in every respect journeying into unknown territory, and at present my only guide was Lady Bellanger.

The winter dark closed in soon after we had finished our lengthy luncheon; we steamed through the unseen countryside, with a welcome break for tea, then looked for station lights until dinner was announced.

Dinner passed as it had done the previous evening, save that the Hungarian officers and Countess Plesch seemed to eat more, to drink more wine and champagne, and to be a little louder in their laughter. Lady Bellanger did not approve, and Captain Talbot looked indifferent. He usually looked indifferent, I thought. Did he have any emotion, any consideration, that stirred or troubled him? If he did, I supposed the soldier in him would surface and crush them. He was not, I decided, a likeable man. He was too cold, too controlled. The Hungarian officers would be better company, even if they were, as Lady Bellanger said, distinctly raffish. I had never known any raffish men.

Then came a silly little incident. The officer in the green tunic, who faced me as we sat at table, was glancing at me now and then with a look of bold interest. Neither Lady Bellanger nor Captain Talbot could see this as they both faced me across our table for four, with their backs to the officers' table. I did my best to ignore it, but it always happens that the more you try to avoid a person's eye the more you seem to meet it, and to talk to my own companions I was forced to look in his direction. At one point he held his glass of champagne and stared at me as if he were toasting me in it. I did not take his attitude as a tribute to my looks; I thought he probably felt obliged to act the audaciously gallant officer, and I, being young and sitting near by, was an easy target. But having a normal amount of vanity I knew that my features were good, my complexion excellent, and my mourning black most becoming to my coppery hair and fair colouring, so there might have been a touch of admiration in it.

We finished our meal before his party, and in leaving had to pass their table. Lady Bellanger went first, and Captain Talbot stood aside for me. The officer in green was sitting by the gangway, and as I passed he moved his hand quickly to emphasise some point in his conversation and touched his champagne glass. It teetered, tipped over, and being half full, poured wine over the tablecloth and splashed a little on the skirt of my gown.

He leapt up with instant apologies, seized a napkin and actually went to brush down my skirt with it. It was firmly twitched from his hand by Captain Talbot, who offered it to me. I gave my skirt one quick wipe and replaced the napkin on the table. By this time, the waiter had appeared with offers of assistance. I thanked him, said it was unnecessary, and walked on without giving the Hungarian another glance. If it had just been an accident, I was still not going to let him profit by it and make my acquaintance. But he was persistent; a few minutes later an attendant brought me a card on which was written,

> To the beautiful young lady in black. My deepest apologies. I kiss your hand in thought, and long to do so in reality. Your devoted servant,
> Palkany Miklas.

When I passed the card to Lady Bellanger, she was loud in condemnation.

'That wretched officer! Such insolence! Of course he did it on purpose to get an introduction, since Captain Talbot had not given him one. A man of *his* reputation! You must be careful, if we should come across him, to keep him well at a distance. A girl like you must have nothing to do with such men!'

Lady Bellanger was distracted from the subject of the officer's behaviour only by the need to get ready to leave the train. Her maid had to be instructed and supervised in the collection and packing of all the toilet articles and odd belongings with which her mistress had passed her time on the journey.

At eleven fifteen precisely the train came to a gentle stop. Outside, the lights flared and defied the darkness; the porters stood ready with their barrows. The carriage doors were flung open, we moved down the carpeted corridor and stepped out on to the platform of the Westbahnhof. I was in Vienna.

CHAPTER TWO

I SLEPT LATE. When I awoke it was daylight, and what was more, the sun was shining.

Lady Bellanger had said that when I was ready for coffee and rolls, I should ring the bell, and I did so. A round-faced, cheerful maid brought delicious coffee and buttery croissants, and asked me in German if I had slept well. When I told her, Yes, she asked,

'Is this your first visit to Vienna, *gnädiges Fräulein*?'

'Yes. I am sure I shall find it interesting.'

'Interesting! *Ja!* You will love Vienna, it is a beautiful city, full of gaiety. And this weather! Nothing like it in November for many, many years. It is just like spring!'

When I was up and dressed, Lady Bellanger sent to ask whether I would like to go for a short drive with her. Nothing would have pleased me better; off we set in her carriage, not needing the heavy wraps we had brought with us.

Lady Bellanger, too, remarked on the weather. 'It is quite incredible—*quite* incredible! So very warm and sunny. My maid tells me that some of the trees in the woods are even trying to bud! In November! Nature is topsy-turvy! We shall pay for it later—when winter comes, it will be a bitter one.'

I could disregard her gloomy forecast as we rattled over the cobbles and I looked round me at all the fine buildings. Sir Thomas and Lady Bellanger lived in the fashionable part of the city, where much had been rebuilt, some imitating baroque architecture, some copying the gothic, but all looking most imposing. The new Ringstrasse was beautiful—splendid buildings along a wide road lined with trees, which in summer must have given delightful shade and perfumed the air with the scent of lime-blossom. Up and down the road passed a variety of smart carriages drawn by glossy, high-stepping horses, driven by liveried coachmen and carrying elegant ladies and gentlemen. There were plenty of riders, too, some civilians, some army officers in uniform, and pedestrians tempted out to stroll in the sun. In the pale golden light it looked, as my maid had said, full of gaiety.

As we drove, I listened to Lady Bellanger with only half an ear, for my mind was turning over my dilemma, my lack of plans, my inability to ask questions when I did not even know what I should ask. After I had seen my father's grave, if I had discovered nothing, what excuse could I make to prolong my stay, and what good would it do if I did? It was no use worrying about it—for the time being, I might as well enjoy the drive. Lady Bellanger went on pointing out places of interest to me.

Our coachman had drawn our carriage to a walking pace at a crossroads, as drivers were obliged to do, when to my surprise a light closed carriage came up beside us at a good speed, and without slowing its pace in the least rattled across and carried on down the road, passing other vehicles and threading its way through with surprising skill and daring. As it passed, I had glimpsed its occupant—a young man in a tweed jacket, with a long pale face and a large fair moustache.

'Well, now, *that* is something!' exclaimed Lady Bellanger. 'Did you see him?'

'Just for a moment.'

'Do you know who it was?'

'No—how should I?'

'There's only one person who can be driven like that, ignoring all the rules! That Bratfisch, thank heaven, is a good coachman! It was the Crown Prince Rudolf, of course!'

'The Crown Prince! But he wasn't in uniform, and the carriage was very plain—no coat of arms on the door, not even a line of colour on the wheel-spokes!'

'That is how he goes about on his private business. But there's no mistaking the way he's driven —all the priorities!'

So that was the Crown Prince Rudolf! I must admit that I was surprised.

Lady Bellanger suddenly realised it was nearly time for luncheon, and ordered the coachman to make a quick return. He touched up the horses, and after a few minutes turned off the main boulevard into a narrower street. Lady Bellanger looked up.

'Not this way, Ernst!' she protested.

'It is the shortest way, m'lady.'

'Oh, very well.'

I could not think what her objection was, except that the streets were much narrower than the Ring. We were still in a very high-class neighbourhood. The houses we were passing were large and dig nified, true baroque, and I looked about me with undiminished pleasure. Lady Bellanger remarked that this was the old town, where the streets were narrow and not laid out to a clear plan. We drove on, through a charming square with a central fountain, and down the street on the far side.

And then I had a surprise—so unexpected that I almost gave myself away. I just managed not to start, and to control the exclamation that sprang to my lips. We were approaching a large building with beautiful ornamentation over the windows, a pillared front and a great central door. And there, over the doorway which was large enough to accommodate a coach-and-four, was carved in the stonework an ornate coat of arms with a phoenix surrounded by flames in the centre—the same coat of arms as that on my father's keepsake.

I looked along the façade. The building ran as far as the next crossroads, with a glassed-in balcony on the first floor running round the corner of the building. The mansion took the whole corner, and was almost as deep as it was long. But—the coat of arms! I must not let this opportunity slip to find out what I could.

'What a splendid building that is,' I said, trying to sound casual. 'Surely it is not a private house?'

'Oh, yes, my dear,' Lady Bellanger answered. 'That is the Phönix Palast. It belongs to a very old Austrian family. The late Baroness Phönix had the title in her own right, before she married Baron Feldbach. When she died, her daughter took over the mother's title, and the Palace now belongs to her. I believe she sometimes stays there, but we never see her.'

'Why not?'

'She has become an invalid, I believe . . . Ah, thank goodness, we are nearly home.'

I thought I had better not rouse Lady Bellanger's curiosity by asking more questions about the Baroness Phönix, though I should have loved to know what sort of person she was. I imagined her as very aristocratic, elderly and frail. Perhaps when she and my father were young they had known each other. Would I ever find out? But the writing on the letter had not been that of an elderly aristocrat.

Luckily Lady Bellanger did not think it necessary to fill in my time after luncheon. She retired to rest, expecting me to do the same. I went to my room, but instead of resting I spent a while in thought. Then I rang the bell for the maid. She was a nice girl, and we had already established good relations, although I found her Viennese accent difficult to follow.

'Tilde, I want to go out,' I said. 'Will you come with me?'

Her eyes widened. 'You'll want the carriage, *Fräulein*?'

'No, I just want to take a little stroll. I find the city so delightful.'

'But . . .' She was uncertain, for this was not according to the strict proprieties. 'But will the *gnädige Frau* approve?'

I smiled. 'The *gnädige Frau* need not know. That would be tactful.'

She smothered a giggle. '*Fräulein*—so soon!'

'Tilde, I am not going to meet a gentleman. I am simply going for a walk.'

She smoothed her face into seriousness, but I

think did not believe me. 'I beg your pardon, *Fräulein*, I did not think . . .'

'You did, but I forgive you. Let us go.'

It seemed much further on foot than I expected, and more than once I thought I had missed my way. Tilde was looking concerned, and ventured,

'*Fräulein*, shouldn't we go back?'

I shook my head, looking for the next crossroad. And there it was, on the next corner, the side of the building with the glazed balcony running round it.

'That building is the Phönix Palast, isn't it?' I asked.

Tilde agreed.

'It is very large!' I went on. 'I wonder how many people live there?'

'Ah, *Fräulein*, we never hear about the family nowadays. Most of them are dead. As for the rest, I don't know where they are—perhaps they don't live there any more.'

It did not seem to me that she had anything to tell me; I felt that my time might be short and I needed to do something positive. But not in front of Tilde.

'Tilde, I think we had better drive home. I shall wait here, while you go round the corner and see if you can find an empty cab.'

'Oh, *Fräulein*, I can't leave you! You cannot stand alone on the pavement! If we wait here, a cab is sure to pass . . .'

'There is a much better chance at the next crossroad. I cannot possibly come to any harm here in two minutes in broad daylight! Please do as I say.'

'Well, if you insist, *Fräulein* . . .'

I silently prayed that a cab would not come along for a few minutes, and hurried up to the door of the

Phoenix Palace. Boldness was the only thing that would serve me. I seized the big wrought-iron bell-pull, and tugged.

I heard the bell ring distantly inside—in the porter's lodge, I supposed. I waited. I pulled again. Oh, come on, come on, I was saying to myself, when I heard a bolt being withdrawn, and a small door inside the huge one opened about six inches.

An elderly man in servant's livery stood inside. He opened the door a little more and looked at me somewhat suspiciously.

'Good afternoon,' I said in my best German. 'Would you please tell me who lives here?'

I was amazed at my own temerity. His look of suspicion deepened.

'Whom did you want?' he retorted.

This is getting me nowhere, I thought, and decided to gamble everything. 'I want to see the person who needs help.'

His grey eyebrows went up, and then a look of comprehension came into his eyes, accompanied, unfortunately, by one of mild contempt.

'Oh, you're one of those religious ladies, are you? Well, *Fräulein*, there's nothing you can do here.'

He made to shut the door, but in desperation I placed my foot inside, and fumbled in my reticule.

'No, I'm not a religious fanatic!' I said urgently. 'Tell me who is here! You can't refuse me a little information, when I have—this.'

I pulled out the gold medallion and dangled it in front of his eyes. It had the effect I wanted. It brought him up in his tracks, and he looked amazed, almost startled. And at that moment I saw another figure. An elderly woman with a wrinkled face and grey hair topped by a servant's cap had crept up behind him, and was looking over his shoulder.

'*Gott in Himmel!*' she exclaimed. 'It's the keep-sake!' She broke off and stared at me. 'Who are you? Why have you come?'

'Let me in!' I said, feeling the precious minutes slipping away, expecting at any moment to see Tilde reappearing. 'Tell me who needs help.'

The man seemed to want to silence her, and began to push her back, but the woman drew in her breath sharply and answered me with sudden urgency.

'It's the Baroness Adèle—but you're . . .' She stopped again, and looked quickly behind her. 'She's coming—that woman—you must go!'

'*Tell me!*' I said insistently.

'There's no time! Come tomorrow—go *now*—go!'

The woman pushed me away. I could hear foot-steps in the distance, the light, sharp footsteps of a woman in fashionable shoes. I did as I was told, and retreated. The door closed quietly behind me.

My heart, I discovered, was beating fast, my hands positively clammy. I thrust the medallion back into my bag and walked quickly down the road as a carriage drew up outside the door. Not a cab, but a smart private carriage—for 'that woman'? I walked on. A cab came towards me, stopped, and Tilde got out.

'Oh, *Fräulein*, I had to wait so long . . .'

As we drove off, I looked out of the window. A man in uniform had got out of the carriage, and greeting the lady who had just come out of the Palace, he handed her up and joined her inside. In that brief moment I recognised them both—it was the Hungarian Palkany, and the Countess Plesch.

To say I was excited by what had happened was to understate the case. I could not doubt that I had stumbled on something relevant to my mystery; the attitude of the old serving-woman told me that there was indeed someone who needed help— the Baroness—and that my possession of the medallion had gained the woman's trust.

I had from the beginning considered that a girl or a woman was involved, for it was most unlikely that a man or even a boy would be driven to appeal for aid to someone in another country. It had to be someone quite helpless, desperate, who could not count on any support from around them, or perhaps had no relatives to turn to. How anyone had come to know, and use, my father's name was the main part of the mystery. And somehow the Countess Plesch was concerned; it was plain that the servant was afraid of her or her influence.

I remembered Lady Bellanger's remark to Captain Talbot, that one day Countess Plesch would go too far . . . What sort of reputation did she have, I wondered. I must keep my ears open. And tomorrow, I told myself, I might hear the complete story and find out how my father came to be involved.

The next morning my plan went completely astray. A messenger from the Embassy called to say that my escort would come at eleven to take me on my sad visit. I had no alternative—it was the one thing I could not excuse myself from. There was no arguing with that. I had been so sure that my journey would be delayed another day, and now the servants at the Palace would think I had let them down. When I did manage to get there, they might be unwilling to talk, and I should be no nearer to discovering anything.

But Lady Bellanger had a headache. It must have been severe, for she decided she could not go with me, and I needed a chaperon. At length she agreed that I could make do with the maid Tilde, whom she had now assigned to me personally.

I was sitting in the drawing-room at two minutes to eleven when the footman announced Captain Talbot. He was back on duty, for he was in full uniform, the scarlet tunic moulded his trim muscular figure, his plumed helmet was carried on one arm, his boots shone like mirrors.

I responded to his greeting, and then said, 'I am sorry, Captain Talbot, but Lady Bellanger is indisposed. She has a severe headache.'

'I regret that, but I have not come to see Lady Bellanger. I am here to escort you.'

He did not look as if the prospect pleased him. Suddenly there flashed into my mind what I had overheard in the Foreign Office. He did not consider it his duty—what was it?—'to dance attendance on a little chit who is indulging in maudlin sentimentality'. He had actually meant *me*! At once I was sure of it.

I could feel a flush of anger rising in my cheeks. The insolent, conceited idiot! If he did not feel like doing a civilised courtesy, he should find somewhere barbaric where he could indulge in some rough fighting. I rose to my feet.

'I regret you find this particular duty so little

to your taste, Captain Talbot,' I said coldly. 'Unfortunately *I* have no choice, either.'

He looked at me questioningly. 'Why, Lady
Charlotte . . .'

'We are in the same boat, Captain, against our
wishes. While you consider me a maudlin sentimental chit, remember that I find you a narrow-
minded, insensitive, conceited—*stick*. Shall we go?'

It was not a good start to our journey. He sat
opposite to me in the carriage—I had Tilde beside
me—and we both fumed in silence. I tried to make
some conversation with Tilde in German—she
spoke no English—asking her about the places we
passed, but she was plainly inhibited by the Captain's presence and answered a mere couple of
words at a time. So we drove through the suburbs of
Vienna and out into the country, the Captain staring poker-faced into the distance, sitting in an
attitude of stiff disapproval; myself, I dare say,
looking cross and haughty; and Tilde trying not to
shoot curious glances at each of us in turn, piqued
into wondering what was going on.

We began to approach the Vienna woods. I
looked at the vines that clothed the hillsides in row
after regular row, and saw the woods rising behind
them, still showing glorious colours of yellow and
russet and red, for the warm weather was delaying
the shedding of their leaves. Below us the fields
were green; above us the sky was pale blue, cloud-
dotted; it was very beautiful. I could not help
smiling as I looked about me. I turned back from
the window and caught Captain Talbot's eye.

At last he spoke, pushing the words out rather
grudgingly. 'Lady Charlotte—may an insensitive

stick apologise for a remark made in ill-temper—a remark which was quite unjustified?'

He was not smiling, and did not look at all apologetic. His grey eyes were very cool, as if he resented the effort it had cost him; and while I was prepared to agree to a truce, I did not intend him to think I was rushing to win his favour.

'You may, Captain Talbot,' I answered. 'That should put us both in a better temper.'

He waited. I am sure he expected me to take back my words, but I did not. I was not going to give him that satisfaction, especially as they were my true opinion.

He leaned back, uncrossed and recrossed his legs. 'I would say it puts us into a state of armed neutrality,' he commented. 'In which case, I trust it will be possible to maintain some conversation.'

I smiled sweetly. 'Quite possible, I should think. You could start by telling me where we are going.'

'We are going to a village which lies some miles beyond Baden. It will take us a little over two hours. We could have taken the train as far as Baden, but we should have had to hire a cab from there, and this is an agreeable drive.'

It certainly was. The carriage was well sprung so that the unevenness of the country road did not make us uncomfortable, and as we bounced along we could hear birdsong above the rattle of wheels and harness and the clopping of hoofs.

'I suggest we stop somewhere near Baden for luncheon,' he went on.

Trust a man to think of that, I said to myself. But that wasn't fair; it would obviously be late if we waited until after I had visited the grave. So we stopped before we reached Baden, at a country inn. There Tilde disappeared with the coachman, and the innkeeper having been told to give them a meal, the Captain and I sat together in a corner of the dining-room at a table covered with a red check cloth, with the antlered head of a deer peering into our soup. I was determined not to be maudlin or sentimental, so I tried to forget all about my father's death.

The deer's head was only one of many trophies around the room, so as we ate some tender Wiener schnitzel, I said, 'This must be hunting country, Captain?'

'Yes. There is plenty of game in those wooded hills. While some people come to Baden for the waters, which taste revoltingly of sulphur and are said to cure a vast number of ills, other people go further on to hunting-lodges and enjoy the shooting. You may have heard that the Crown Prince has a hunting-lodge at Mayerling.'

'I haven't been here long enough to hear anything, but I did catch a glimpse of him in his carriage. He looked rather thin and bored.'

Captain Talbot actually laughed. 'What a summing-up of such an august personage! Practically *lèse-majesté*! But not too wide of the mark.'

'But why on earth should he be bored? In his position, I should think he could do anything.'

The Captain considered this. 'No. He can have anything—except the one thing he wants. He can do everything that is unimportant, and nothing that really matters to him.'

'You seem to know a lot about him, Captain. Please explain?'

'I know very little, but one can make observations. I believe he wants to have some power in government, and of course he has none. The Emperor delegates nothing, and, what is more, he is rigidly set in his opinions and ways. If Prince Rudolf believes the Empire should be changing, he can do nothing about it. It is beneath him to indulge in political intrigue, he has little scope for his intelligence—and I think he is no fool—so there is little left for him but idle amusements. It is not surprising that he takes his pleasures sadly.'

'And what are his pleasures?' I asked.

On looking back I know I was ridiculously innocent—what a question!

The Captain shot me a piercing look. 'Those of any young aristocrat. May I give you a little more wine? Do you like this? It is the new wine.'

'It is delicious—thank you.'

So we went on chatting, quite pleasantly, until the meal was over and we were all three seated once more in the carriage.

We drove through Baden, with Captain Talbot like a good escort pointing out to me the eighteenth-century plague column and the fifteenth-century parish church of St Stephen with its baroque spire, and then we left the town behind and began to drive through the Helenen valley into more wooded country. After a few more miles and a couple of ruins we turned on to a narrower road that ran along the side of a hill. Soon we were travelling through a cleft between steeply rising wooded slopes; I could hear an invisible stream rushing along somewhere below us, and a few minutes later we rounded a spur, and the land opened out into a kind of saucer in which were clustered a number of farms and houses. To one side a little grey church pointed the finger of its spire above the rooftops. The Captain craned round to look.

'Ah—you can see Marienwald now,' he said.

The walled cemetery stood some way apart from the church on the side of the hill. At the sound of our carriage-wheels, a woman came out of a near-by house, bearing the key to the cemetery gate. The Captain spoke to her and she let us in. She led the way, I followed, and Captain Talbot walked a pace or two behind. One could see that the community here was not wealthy; although there were some ornate memorials there were many more plain tombs, and some green mounds had no stone at all.

We reached a far corner, and there by itself was a grave which was newer than the rest. It was covered by a plain slab of marble which bore, as I had instructed, my father's name, the dates of his birth and death, the letters RIP, and nothing more. At the sight of it, realisation struck me harder than ever before that I should never see him again. The knowledge that he had thrown away his life on some quixotic mission about which he had told me nothing made it even harder to bear. I stood by the graveside and tried to pray, but all that came was, 'Oh, God, why did you let it happen?'

The woman had left us, and an old priest was hurrying in our direction through the lines of graves. When he reached us, he greeted Captain Talbot by name, and then said,

'And this is the young lady? My child, this is a sad journey for you. I trust in God that it will bring you consolation.'

I am not very religious: what consolation can anyone get out of seeing a grave? I wondered. But I thanked him as best I could. My throat was tightening, and tears were filling my eyes and beginning to run down my cheeks. I mustn't cry, I said to myself, not in front of Captain Talbot. But I could not help it, and I went on standing there, trying to check my tears, wiping my eyes, snuffling a little and wishing desperately I had not come. It only made everything worse.

The old priest began quietly to pray beside me, and I did my best to join in. Somehow it helped me to gain control. He stopped, and waited. I nodded, and we left the graveside. Captain Talbot had moved some way ahead of us; he left the cemetery and went towards the carriage. The old priest, with his white hair lifting in the light breeze, and his stooped figure, turned his head and looked at me in sympathy. Beside the cemetery wall a rowan tree was growing, its red berries a gleaming splash of colour. On an impulse I reached up and with some difficulty broke off a spray. I had not thought to order a wreath to bring, it seemed so morbid; but this simple branch was somehow fitting. I went back to my father's grave and laid it on the slab. The berries shone there like drops of blood.

The priest had come back with me, and as I stood for a moment with bowed head, he took my hand in his and murmured, 'God will help you, my child. He always gives the strength when He gives a burden. Such a sad accident, but it must be part of His pattern.'

The word struck me—'accident'. Had I misunderstood his German? Surely he would not call the fever an accident?

'Father,' I asked. 'Did you say "accident"?'

He looked at me, a trifle confused, and I went on. 'What did you mean, father?'

He pressed my hand in his. 'Of course it was an accident, my child. You did not think he had . . . ? Oh, no, quite impossible. It was a hunting accident. He was shot from some distance, I know.'

I gazed at him, for the moment stupefied. *Shot!* He patted my hand comfortingly, his eyes sad and kindly in his pink, wrinkled face.

'Oh, no, not suicide, my dear—why ever should you think that?'

'Father,' I said woodenly, 'I was told he died of typhoid fever.'

'Oh, my poor, poor child! Now I have added to your burden. No doubt it was thought a kinder thing to tell you. What an old fool I am. Now I remember—the officer warned me not to talk to you about the death . . .'

'You did right to tell me, Father,' I said firmly. 'I had to know. You are sure—quite sure—it was not fever?'

He was shaking his head. 'Dear me, I am a foolish old man! But I am sure of that. I saw his body. No, my child, he had been shot. It was an accident in the woods. The man was most distressed . . .'

'What man?'

His hand began to tremble, he looked confused.

'The man—I suppose the man who shot him—or perhaps he just found the body. I really don't know.'

'But who was he?'

'A stranger. I did not know him. My child, this is

what everyone wanted to avoid for you. No one was to blame—you must try to forget it.'

He was getting upset, and I had not the heart to press him. And Captain Talbot was turning back to us.

'We'll say nothing more of it,' I assured him, and then I did something which was for me quite uncharacteristic. 'Please give me your blessing, Father.' I dropped to my knees beside the grave, unable to bear the sight of those blood-red berries.

I said very little on the drive back. I did not weep, but sat, stony-faced. Well, he cannot call me maudlin, I thought, though he can put my silence down to grief. In fact my mind was in a tumult, turning over what I had discovered. It had been a shock, and it was an added shock to realise that there had been a conspiracy going back as far as the Foreign Office in London—for it was from there I had been told that my father had died of typhoid fever. Unless, of course, that was information they had taken on trust. But surely the Embassy here must know the facts? Surely some official would see the body of a British subject who died abroad? Was that why Captain Talbot had been detailed as my escort? The priest had met him before, and had been told by him not to discuss my father's death. The Captain had stuck pretty closely to us to make sure—if I had not gone back with the spray of berries, he would have prevented the disclosure. He had not reckoned on that, or on the priest joining me to give me consolation.

Let him think that was all that passed between us. If I were going to find out anything more, I felt it would not be through Captain Talbot. Now I thought of a way of testing this.

'Grief must have affected my power of thought,' I said to him. 'I have just realised that I have been very remiss.'

'Remiss? In what way?'

'My father died of fever in that village. Someone must have nursed him. And I have no idea who it was—I should have found out, and gone to thank them.'

His face showed no reaction. 'Oh, were you not told?' he said smoothly. 'It was all very sudden —the village nurse took him in, and he died within two days. She has since left the village and gone to live with relatives—in Italy, I believe. But I can assure you she was thanked by the Embassy and paid, quite generously, for her nursing.'

You weren't here, I thought. Is that what you were told and you believe it, or do you know the truth and are lying to me? For a moment I toyed with the idea of telling him I now knew how my father had died. And where would that get me? He was a man under discipline, he would stick to his story, whether he believed it or not, for that was the official line. And if he did know the truth, he would immediately pass the warning that I had found out what it was intended to keep from me. No, Captain Talbot, I thought. I do not trust you. For that matter, I do not trust anybody.

I knew from that moment that the mystery of the keepsake was real, and serious, and that I would have to work alone. Yet even then my conceit was such that it did not occur to me to see that I might be inviting personal danger. The knowledge of that only came much later.

CHAPTER THREE

LADY BELLANGER could not have been kinder. It was simply ironic that just at the time when I was most anxious to be left alone to pursue my own private business, she decided I needed distracting and that every moment must be filled. So I was taken on a steady round of social engagements. Nothing too frivolous, of course; but to my surprise she insisted that I must not be too rigid about mourning.

'After all, some months have passed since your father's death. You are very young, and Vienna itself is not too lighthearted at present, with the Court in mourning—though not the deepest degree, I am glad to say—for the Empress's father.'

That explained the preponderance of dark toilettes, so many gowns of black and grey, with jet and pearls; for where the Court led, everyone followed.

We went to private parties, a concert and a serious play, and Lady Bellanger pointed out to me the important figures in society, including the latest leader of fashion, the Baroness Mary Vetsera, a handsome dark-eyed girl wearing sables. And where we went, sooner or later, Captain Talbot would appear. He was most polite, most correct, and yet I thought there was a sardonic gleam in those grey eyes whenever he looked at me.

I told myself that it was possible that I was

imagining everything. There might be no sinister reason at all for the misreporting of my father's death: it could be exactly as the priest had said, that it was intended to spare me pain. Fever could be accepted as a natural hazard; death in a hunting accident immediately aroused feelings of blame and resentment at someone's criminal carelessness. No one had nursed my father, for the priest had spoken of finding the body, but the Captain's tale of a nurse who had since left the village could still be part of the intention to stop me from probing into a situation which for my sake was best left alone. I decided that outwardly, at least, I would accept the fiction.

I could not so easily ignore the mystery of the medallion. Ten times a day it would come to my mind that someone needed help, and that I had failed to return to the Phoenix Palace. I even considered taking Lady Bellanger into my confidence, but I knew only too well what her reactions would be—'My dear Charlotte, you cannot possibly interfere in the affairs of perfect strangers on such a flimsy pretext! Your imagination is running away with you!' So I had to endure her kindess and fall in with all her social arrangements. When I suggested that I was being a trouble to her, she warmly contradicted me and said it was a pleasure to have young company.

'I do hope you will stay for Christmas? You have no reason to rush back to England, and you have not seen Vienna at her best. Of course, in January there is Carnival—now that is really worth waiting for!'

I thanked her, not feeling in the least like

enjoying Carnival, or even Christmas without my father.

It was nearly a week before I found myself with a free afternoon. I knew it would be quite shocking for me to slip out of the house alone—everyone would think I was going on some assignation, for such affairs were the main preoccupation in Vienna, as far as I could judge—but that was what I must do. I had to go to the Phoenix Palace, and that without telling a soul.

So, feeling very daring, that was what I did, muffled up in a cloak, hat and veil, and hoping to be unrecognised. I was lucky to find an empty cab at the end of the street, and I told the driver to take me to a church which was along the road by the Palace. When we reached there, I paid him, went into the church by the main door and out by a side one; from there I walked quickly to the Palace.

I rang the bell. There was no answer. I rang again, anxiety gnawing at me—had I come for nothing? After an age of waiting, I heard the bolt being withdrawn. The old man was inside.

I lifted my veil.

'Oh, it's you!' he said. 'We thought you'd forgotten.'

I heard shuffling steps, and saw the woman behind him.

'Please let me in,' I said. 'I'm sorry I couldn't come before—it wasn't possible. But I must know what is happening.'

She didn't answer at once; then she turned to the man and said, 'There's nothing *we* can do, Gottlieb. Perhaps the *Fräulein* . . .'

Grudgingly he opened the door, and I stepped inside.

It was so dark that at first I could see nothing. Then, as my eyes became used to it, I became aware that I was in a huge hall, square and stone-flagged, very lofty, from one side of which rose a great stone staircase with carved figures of fantastic beasts on the newel-posts and at intervals up the balustrade. There were one or two lamps burning on the walls, and no other light; it was indescribably gloomy. Once, perhaps, it had been lit by torchlight or hundreds of candles, and coaches had lumbered in, and people in multi-coloured silks and satins had mounted that wide staircase. But now it was dark, silent, gloomy—and very cold. I shivered, and pulled my cloak about me.

'Come in here,' said the woman, and hurried me into what seemed in comparison a large cupboard beside the door. It was the porter's lodge, with a table, a few plain wooden chairs, and a stove—an old-fashioned stove—but thank heaven it was alight and glowing, and giving a very pleasant warmth into the little room. On the table was an empty coffee-cup, a plate with a few crumbs, and a copy of the *Wiener Tagblatt*—all very normal.

The woman placed a chair for me. 'Who are you?' she asked bluntly.

They both stood in front of me, staring down into my face. I was not afraid of them, as I had no reason to be, and I did not think they were hostile, but they were certainly very wary, and probably nervous.

'My name is Charlotte Brantham. Does that mean anything to you?'

She repeated it slowly, as best she could, and

then said, 'Are you *his* daughter?'

'My father was Lord Hilary Brantham.'

'*Was?*' she said slowly. 'So it is true—he is dead . . .'

'Yes. That is why I am here.'

'He asked you?' she gasped incredulously.

'No. I thought . . .'

'Why should you come?' the man Gottlieb interrupted roughly. 'He did nothing.'

'He was trying to!' I retorted sharply. 'For heaven's sake, if you need help, at least tell me what is going on!'

The woman's mouth trembled; she put her hand to her face and started to cry, silently, despairingly. Gottlieb took her by the shoulders and sat her down, not unkindly.

'*Please!*' I implored. 'Tell me from the beginning. I know nothing, except that my father had an appeal for help.'

'I sent that,' she sobbed. 'It was our last hope. My young mistress tried to write, but the Baroness her stepmother caught her and tore the letter up. Then she took all writing things away. But I found some of the pieces, and knew the English milord would recognise the coat of arms. I'm not good at writing, you understand, but I remembered the address my sweet lady had taught me. So I wrote "Help" on the piece of paper with the crest, put the name and address on an envelope and posted it. It was all I could do.'

'It worked very well,' I told her. 'It brought my father here.'

My mind was trying to adjust itself, for she had said 'young mistress'.

'But why did your mistress need help?' I asked.

'They are trying to force her to marry!'

'Who are "they"?'

'The Baroness her stepmother, and *her*—that Countess Plesch. *And* Count Palkany—and that Szarvas, who intends to marry her . . .'

Countess Plesch—and Palkany! My pulses quickened.

'But the marriage—would it be so dreadful? And how can they force her?'

'Oh, you don't know! You don't know! It is all to get control of the money the Baron left her—she was the only child—and they will do *anything* to get it.'

'How old is she?'

'Not yet twenty-one. At twenty-one she can marry without permission, but she cannot handle the money until she is twenty-five. And, of course, when she marries, the husband has control.'

'Before she is twenty-five?'

'At once.' She made a despairing gesture. 'So, you see, they try to force her now.'

'Force her! But she has only to refuse, and keep on refusing!'

'Oh, you do not know how things are! They will be too much for her. Already their tormenting has made her ill—she does not eat . . .'

'How did my father come into this? I do not know how he could ever have seen your mistress since she was a tiny child. I do not think he could have known her . . .'

The old woman looked at me, suddenly wary.

'No, but he—he once knew her mother. That was before she married the Baron. That marriage was a family arrangement. She gave your father's name and address to young Baroness Adèle . . .'

Now I understood. My father and the girl's mother—a keepsake had passed between them —she had married, and he had never returned to Vienna. I took the medallion out of my bag and turned it over and over in my hand. For some time now I had known what the one word engraved upon it meant. One word in German script— '*Erinnerung*'—'Remembrance'.

'So her mother gave my father this keepsake?' I said. 'They had been sweethearts?'

'Sweethearts—yes. But marriage was impossible. She had been promised to the Baron for more than a year.'

'So my father went away. I suppose he told her that if she ever needed help, she must let him know?'

'Yes—but she died five years ago, my dear, dear mistress. I knew about the English milord, although it was long ago, for I was her maid then. So the milord married, too—and you are his daughter,' she added thoughtfully.

I dragged my mind away from the past, back to the present. 'And now the young Baroness is ill? What does the doctor say? She must have a doctor? If she told him, couldn't he prevent her being forced to marry?'

'The doctor! He knows nothing! When he comes, they are full of love and anxiety, and the Baroness Feldbach would deny any suggestion of pressing a marriage—they say she is imagining it.'

'So what is to be done?' I said, more to myself than her, for I saw no way of intervening.

'Now the English milord is dead, there is nothing anyone can do.'

I was thinking that I was a fool to come, the woman might be making a mountain out of a molehill, and she was right, there really was nothing I could do.

But now something else occurred to her, and she clutched my arm. 'We heard of the death, but not how he died. Do you know?'

'He was shot in a hunting accident,' I said bluntly.

She gazed at me, her eyes widening in horror, and said one word, *'Where?'*

'Near a village beyond Baden, called Marienwald.'

'Marienwald . . .' she repeated slowly. *'Gott in Himmel!'* Suddenly she was frightened. 'It is best for you to go now! You cannot help my lady.'

'What do you know about Marienwald?'

'Nothing! Nothing! You must go. Do not come again. You have been very kind, but now you must go. Go away and forget us.'

A wall had risen between us: neither of them would say anything more. They hurried me out of the room, and practically thrust me out of the door. With my mind in confusion and my eyes momentarily dazzled by the pale sunshine, I walked away, almost into the arms of a passer-by.

I drew back, and looked up into a face I recognised. High cheekbones, a narrow jaw, eyes nearly as black as his hair and moustache, a wide thin mouth: it was the officer with the wolf-skin. He smiled and saluted me, then bowed for good measure.

'*Gnädiges Fräulein!* I am indeed fortunate to meet you! Pray allow me to accompany you along the street.'

Being alone, I had only one defence. I looked him full in the eyes and replied to his flowery Viennese phrases slowly, loudly, and in English.

'Go away! I do not speak German!'

'Oh, most charming lady, I am sure you do. Pray take my arm; we will find a fiacre at the crossroads.'

The thought of being alone in a cab with him did not appeal to me in the least. I gave him one long withering look and began to walk away.

Unfortunately he did not wither, but fell into step beside me. 'So you are acquainted with the Baroness?'

I did not answer, but thinking to myself that I must get a cab and make it plain to the driver that I do not want this officer's company, I walked faster. That was very silly of me, as I had no hope of shaking him off. With his long legs, he was practically strolling beside me as I hurried along, and I merely made myself look ridiculous.

'Surely there is no hurry, beautiful *Fräulein*?'

I was hot with embarrassment. It was my own fault for coming out without a maid; seeing me alone, he thought I was fair game.

'How far do you intend to walk, *fräulein*? You English ladies are so athletic—but surely a cab would be more comfortable?'

I began to feel desperate. We had nearly reached the church . . . should I go inside? But would that do any good? The church was probably deserted, and certainly dark . . . Then I looked round, and saw salvation in a strange disguise coming towards me. Walking along from the church steps was Captain Talbot. For once I was glad to see him. He came up to us, and irrationally I found myself thinking, How unfair it is—two men in gorgeous uniforms, and I am looking like a little crow in black! But the thought quickly passed as the Captain reached us.

'Good afternoon, Lady Charlotte. Good afternoon, Palkany. I trust you are not going to make a habit of annoying English ladies in the street?' He was smiling and speaking quite teasingly, and added, 'Surely you have enough scope in the drawing-rooms?'

'Ah, Captain Talbot!' the other replied smoothly. 'Your English wit amazes me! I am simply helping this young lady to find a cab, since she is alone.'

'Your gallantry is now unnecessary, Count—for I am here.'

He offered me his arm, and with considerable relief I took it.

'In that case, Captain, pray introduce me to your charming compatriot.'

'Certainly. Lady Charlotte, may I present Count Miklas Palkany? Palkany, this is Lady Charlotte Brantham.'

For a second, a look flashed between us. I already knew what the old woman had said, that he was the man involved in the plot to force the Baroness to marry, but did he guess I knew? To him, I believed, my name was familiar—too familiar. He realised his look had given him away. He smoothed it over by admitting the knowledge.

'My dear lady—did I not see in the paper that an

English gentleman of your name died here a while ago? Not a relative, I hope?'

'He was my father.'

'How sad. Allow me to offer you my deepest sympathies.'

The black eyes glittered inscrutably. They did not look sympathetic. He knows something about it, I thought. I am sure of that. I did not know what to say or do.

Captain Talbot settled the matter for me. 'And now we really must go. Good afternoon, Palkany.'

My hand felt extraordinarily feeble on his arm, which was hard and steady as a rock. For several paces we walked in silence. Then, feeling very relieved and a little ashamed of myself, I said, 'Thank you, Captain Talbot.'

'Lady Charlotte, you have given me a great deal of pleasure. That fellow thinks he is one of the greatest gallants in the city; I enjoyed besting him.'

I digested the fact that he had done it, not for my relief but for his own gratification, and he went on, 'It is very naughty of you to come out without a maid. If the Count had not accosted you, someone else would have done so.'

As he spoke, he gave a commanding gesture to a cab, which rattled to a stop beside us. He handed me in, and followed. I now began to feel cross. I had made a fool of myself, and been unable to cope in a simple situation.

'You make Vienna sound a disagreeable place for a woman on her own,' I said.

'Disagreeable? Oh, no. Flirtations are the breath of life to Viennese. Women expect to be pursued by men, and men expect to be tantalised—and occasionally rewarded. But you must play by the rules. And rule number one: any young lady who goes about unaccompanied is inviting attention. It is not so very different in England.'

'In England,' I said tartly, 'men usually take "No" for an answer.'

He smiled at me and shook his head. 'It doesn't do to rely on that anywhere. You must know that some men find a trim figure, a beautiful skin, and hair that particular shade of dark gold very attractive.'

Now I was furious. The cool effrontery of the man—cataloguing my good points to my very face and at the same time managing to imply that they held no charm for *him*! And speaking to me as if he were a well-intentioned uncle reproving me and giving advice!

'I did not think a *gentleman* mentioned a lady's —appearance—to her in that way.'

'Which way would you prefer?'

I could have slapped his face.

'At your age, Captain, I suppose you have had time both to learn and to forget the polite way to pay a compliment.'

He leaned back in his seat as we swayed over the cobbles, and sighed. 'Ah, yes. And I am so decrepit, so doddering, I don't know a pretty woman when I see one. I'll have to take Palkany's opinion that you are a beautiful *Fräulein*.'

I had asked for that, which made me even more angry. I couldn't think of a single crushing retort, and anything I said would only betray the fact that he had succeeded in making me lose my temper. So

I said nothing, and we bowled along the boulevard, myself seething, the Captain looking about with bland indifference. What was more, he managed to infuriate me further as we arrived at Lord Bellanger's house. As it came into view, he leaned forward to me and said seriously,

'Lady Charlotte, I hope this will not be too distasteful to you . . .'

'What is it?' I asked.

'The two of us arriving in a cab—yourself heavily veiled, and without a maid—it is bound to give rise to conjecture . . .'

'*Conjecture?*'

'Among the servants, tongues will wag, and word may spread elsewhere, that you and I, Lady Charlotte, have had a secret, a romantic, meeting.'

For the second time I longed to smack his face because he was looking so calm and grave as he made the ridiculous suggestion, but his eyes were mocking me.

'Oh!' I gasped. I was beyond speech.

'Yes, there is no justice. People's imaginations run away with them. Here am I, old and cold and not your type at all—and they will not realise that you can't stand the sight of me and that while we have been alone I haven't once attempted to kiss you.'

If I had had an answer, there would have been no time for it, since the cab had stopped. I gathered the last shreds of my dignity around me and swept indoors, with the aggravating feeling that Captain Talbot was laughing at me all the time.

For a while my rage against the infuriating man drove everything else out of my mind; it was only

later that I recalled what had been said at the
Phoenix Palace, and wondered if I should ever find
out anything more about Baroness Adèle. And
then I remembered Count Palkany and Countess
Plesch, who were playing some part in her misfor-
tunes. And it was possible that the Count had taken
a share in mine, for I was certain he knew something about my father's death.

I was back to thinking about that again.

It wouldn't do, I decided. There seemed to be no
help I could give in the matter that had brought him
here, but I was entitled to find out all I could about
his death, and there was a possible way of doing
that. If I went to Marienwald again and talked to
the priest, he could put me in touch with the police
or whatever representative of the law there might
be in the area of the village, who must have been
called in when my father was found. They could not
refuse to give me some details. There was a disturbing feeling growing within me that the death might
not have been an accident. So I must find out the
circumstances.

I wondered about going on my own, but com-
monsense showed me that it was impracticable. So
I had to turn to Lady Bellanger. I simply told her
that I wanted to visit Marienwald again, and asked
if it would be possible.

After a few moments' hesitation, she agreed. 'Of
course. I shall be glad to come with you. It is a
pleasant drive, and I dare say Captain Talbot would
escort us.'

'There is no need to bother him,' I said rather too
quickly.

'But we must have a man with us—so much more

convenient over luncheon—and should there be any emergency . . .'

It was no good arguing. I was going to be saddled with Captain Talbot again.

It was soon arranged, and I found myself one evening looking forward with very mixed feelings to the following day. It would be harrowing, discussing the manner of my father's death; it might be shocking, too; and undoubtedly it would be very irritating to spend several hours in the company of Captain Talbot. I did not relish the journey, and I was nervous about the rest of the business.

But plans can go astray without warning, and so did mine.

That night the weather changed. The amazingly warm period finished as quickly and unaccountably as it had begun: the temperature plummeted, and by morning Vienna was clothed inches deep in snow.

CHAPTER FOUR

AT FIRST I still hoped we might make our journey. The train, Lady Bellanger said, would certainly run to Baden, although there might be delays. At this my hopes rose, but she continued,

'I cannot see any cabman agreeing to take a fare from there to Marienwald, but I will find out what I can.'

A manservant was sent out, and returned depressingly quickly, with news gleaned heaven-knows-where. Word had come by telegraph that snowfalls had been heavy everywhere; more was on the way; the country roads would be in a bad state.

It would be utter folly to attempt the journey, Lady Bellanger decided. Then Captain Talbot arrived and reinforced her decision.

'I have no wish to be snowbound in the mountains,' he said, 'so may I suggest another form of amusement? Vienna is transformed: shall we go for a drive and see it under snow? And the *Christkindlmarkt* is in full swing—Lady Charlotte might find that a novelty.'

Since I had to give in, I did so with a good grace. Lady Bellanger and I wrapped ourselves warmly, put on hats and gloves and picked up our muffs, and the Captain escorted us to the carriage which by now was ready for us. He was quite right—Vienna was transformed.

The snow in the streets, though marked by

wheels and feet, had not degenerated into slush; everywhere there was a white carpet; snow lay on rooftops, the cornices of buildings and the boughs of the trees along the streets; in the Ringstrasse the monuments all wore white fur helmets and stood in mounds of cotton wool. The cabbies, while waiting for fares at their stands, were keeping themselves amused and active by building snowmen, to the delight of the children who had dragged their nursemaids out to see the fun.

'They are building the Skaters' Palace at the Eislaufverein,' the captain told us. 'We shall soon be able to skate, for this weather is going to hold.' He turned to me. 'Do you skate, Lady Charlotte?'

'Not at all well,' I replied. 'In fact, I still fall over rather easily.'

He laughed. 'Then we must give you some practice. But today we will go to Am Hof.'

'Am Hof?' I queried.

'The square where the *Christkindlmarkt* is held.'

'And whatever is that?'

'Wait and see. I hope you will be surprised.'

I repeated the name to myself—surely I had translated it correctly? The Little Christ Child's Market? What could it be?

I soon found out. It was like walking into a fairy-tale, and finding one's self a large human being among tiny fairy-folk. The square was full of little cabins, child-size, doll-size, and the cabins were full of toys. There were lovely dolls with waxen faces and flaxen hair dressed in frills and laces, dolls in uniform, dolls like fairies and angels, a whole population of dolls; tin soldiers and toy forts, with cannon ready and banners flying; jumping-jacks and jacks-in-the-box; hopping frogs and bouncing rabbits; puzzles and puppets, marionettes and monkeys, ballerinas, and firemen in brass helmets. Then there were more ephemeral treasures—great piles of candy, boxes of biscuits, heaps of nuts with gilded shells, and masses of gingerbread baked in different disguises.

We had, of course, left the carriage and were walking among the stalls. 'Do you like it?' said Captain Talbot to me.

I did not try to hide my delight; he could think me childish if he wished. 'I love it!' I said, laughing with pleasure. 'And I am going to buy a gingerbread man, and shock you by eating it now!'

Lady Bellanger did not look at all shocked; I had found that beneath her formality there was a very soft heart. 'I think such convention has gone by the board here,' she said.

By the gingerbread stall was a group of three children, unaccompanied: they could have been a brother and two sisters, poorly dressed, rather pale and pinched, with wide, longing eyes. It was plain they had no money for the gingerbread they yearned for.

I bought four gingerbread men, and gave them one each. They were speechless with amazement and delight.

'Go on, eat them up!' I said, and started on my own. Their little faces broke into smiles, smiles which were soon covered with gingerbread crumbs.

'I am sure you got your money's worth of pleasure out of that,' remarked Captain Talbot.

His eyes as well as his lips were smiling, and this

time there was no mockery in them. He returned to me a glove I had dropped when paying for the gingerbread, and we went back to the carriage.

We drove through a Vienna which was suddenly preparing for Christmas. Overnight, it seemed, with the snow had come the Christmas trees—their green was everywhere; and the shop windows were full of beautiful, expensive gifts. What did it matter if the Court was in partial mourning? Vienna was going to have a merry Christmas.

I remember that day very well, for it was a day of surprises. Surprise at the snow, which greeted me on waking; surprise at the Captain, that he should think of showing me the Toy Market and a transformed Vienna.

Nevertheless I could not keep more serious matters out of my mind. Being thwarted in my projected trip to Marienwald, my thoughts returned to the young Baroness. The servants had implied that she had been made ill by being worried and tormented, and then there was the business of the letter. The girl had felt sufficiently menaced to write begging for help—to a stranger—and had been prevented. Had the woman not said the letter had been torn up and the writing materials taken away? She could not have imagined that, and she thought it so serious that she had sent the crested letterhead to my father, appealing in the only way she knew. That was a fact—the only solid fact I had to go on. It was enough to convince me I would never be satisfied until I had seen the Baroness Adèle and heard from her lips that she was not under any kind of duress. But how on earth could I manage that?

Only, I at last decided, by being completely unconventional. I had no means of getting an *entrée* to the Phoenix Palace; I had not even a letter of introduction. Very well, I must employ what would be considered by the Viennese a typical piece of English aristocratic high-handedness. Very carefully I composed a short letter to the Baroness Adèle, simply saying that on visiting Vienna and realising that my family in the past had had some acquaintance with members of her family, it would give me great pleasure if she would allow me to call on her.

Of course, the moment it was despatched I began to have qualms. Lady Bellanger, I knew, would be horrified at my presumption; I consoled myself by thinking it was not likely I should even receive an answer, in which case she need never know. I was a fool to have written; if the servant's tale were true, the letter would never even reach the Baroness. And without an answer, what could I do? By writing, I had put the stepmother on her guard. And now, all I could do was wait.

And while I waited I discovered that Captain Talbot had yet another surprise for me. He appeared at the house the following morning, swinging in one hand a pair of skating boots.

'Well, Lady Charlotte, are you coming with me to the Skaters' Palace?'

I was tempted. 'I haven't any boots or skates.'

'No matter—we can hire some.'

I began to give in. 'I skate very badly.'

'I shall stop you from falling and teach you to skate better.'

I succumbed.

The Skaters' Palace was an architectural oddity, like a large villa with cross-timbered turrets, and in front of it was an expanse of ice, which by the time we reached it was already crowded with skaters. The air was cold and crisp, and I was glad of the little fur hat and muff I had brought out for the first time. The Captain was in a cheerful, tolerant mood: he gave me a steadying hand as I moved rather erratically with the other beginners round the edge of the ice, encouraging me and giving me confidence. I struck out, and did quite well—for me; and when I came to grief and nearly fell he caught me in his arms and laughed, not at me but with me. For a moment his face was very close, his clear eyes looked into mine, his smile was warm, and I forgot he was my senior by about twelve years—he looked so young. He was also very strong; he held me as if I were a doll and put me on my feet again.

When he thought I had skated enough he bought roasted chestnuts from a man with a portable brazier that was sending out clouds of black smoke and spreading the most delicious smell. The chestnuts acted as hand-warmers too; they were so hot from the fire that we had to keep our gloves on to eat them. By that time we were not alone; we had been joined by some of Captain Talbot's friends from the Embassy.

I remarked that I wondered how the Embassy managed to function in their absence, and they laughed. 'We have all learnt the art of fitting in our quite unnecessary work between our necessary amusements!' one of them said.

'We can always call this sort of thing "improving

relations",' the Captain added.

'I had an improving relation,' said one young secretary thoughtfully. 'An aunt—she was always trying to improve me. I disliked her intensely.'

'She didn't succeed very well!' someone commented.

'On the contrary. You do not know what I was like before!' he replied in a sad drawl.

They protested when the Captain said it was time he took me home. It had all been such fun.

The very next day I had a reply from the Phoenix Palace. It said: 'The Baroness Feldbach and the Baroness Phönix will be At Home at 4 p.m., and will be pleased to see you.' The time given was the following afternoon.

I showed the card to Lady Bellanger, for it gave no indication that I had written first.

'How extraordinary! And how gracious of them! But why should they?'

'They must have heard from an acquaintance of yours that I am staying with you, and remembered that my father once knew the family.'

I was quite ashamed of my deceit, especially when it satisfied my good hostess.

'Yes, that must be so.'

That afternoon Lady Bellanger lent me her carriage, and I set off alone to the Phoenix Palace. The huge doors were still closed, so the coachman stopped at the pavement, but when he rang the bell, the wicket was opened at once and Gottlieb even managed a rough bow as he showed me inside and handed me over to a liveried footman.

Although a few lamps had been lit, the hall was

still very dark and cold, but I had by now heard that nearly all Viennese mansions of the same period were like that, so it no longer seemed sinister, and I was so pleased to have been invited that I could have patted the strange stone beasts on the balustrade as I ascended the magnificent staircase.

At the top of the stairs we turned left, and the footman showed me into a huge reception room with a patterned marble floor, panelled walls with gilded decoration, overhung with cut-glass chandeliers and sparsely dotted with furniture which, to me, looked more decorative than comfortable. The great porcelain stove that towered in one corner was alight, but its heat could not penetrate far into the vast room. On we went, through another very similar room, and I had still not seen another human being or even the trace of one. The footman opened a door to one side, announced my name, and stood back to let me in.

All at once everything was changed. Compared with the previous two, this room was small. The decoration was similar, and the furniture, too, but now it was intimate rather than grand. The shutters must have been closed over the windows, for the heavy damask curtains were drawn and there were no draughts; the stove had all its own way, filling the room with cosy warmth. Two sofas and some armchairs were placed in a semi-circle round the stove. On one sofa a girl who looked little older than myself was reclining, wearing a négligé and covered from the waist down with a fine fur rug. Her dark brown hair was prettily arranged; she had an oval face with fine features, but she was pale, almost pinched in appearance. In the corner of the other sofa sat a lady I judged to be in her late thirties or early forties, whom I guessed to be the Baroness Feldbach. She was blonde, inclined to plumpness and rather doll-like in looks. She wore a deep blue silk gown which billowed about her, so that she sat in a nest of ruffles and ribbons. In the background stood a parlourmaid in a black dress, frilly white apron and beribboned cap, beside a laden tray.

The blonde lady stood up and came towards me, offering me her hand. 'I must introduce myself. I am the Baroness Feldbach.'

I responded, and she went on to introduce the girl as 'my stepdaughter Adèle—Baroness Phönix'.

The young Baroness smiled at me and held out her hand, and I moved over and took it. It was slim and cold and limp, but as I momentarily blocked her from the view of her stepmother she grasped my fingers with a sudden violent pressure, and her look changed to one of desperate appeal. As I murmured my conventional greeting, I tried to make my smile look encouraging and understanding. When I moved away, she smoothed her features into a formal smile.

Baroness Feldbach offered me a seat beside her, and then tossed over her shoulder the instruction to the maid that she might make the tea.

'We were most interested, Lady Charlotte, to hear that a member of your family was acquainted with that of my late husband. May I ask who it could be?'

'My father,' I answered. 'My late father.'

Out of the corner of my eye I saw Adèle's hand

suddenly clutch at the rug on which it lay. I went on explaining, thinking it best to be as truthful as I dared, for I could not guess how much the Baroness Feldbach knew.

'He was visiting Austria a few months ago, and died here. His death was most sudden. His letters to me had not said whether he had called on you, so I thought I would repair the omission if he had not done so.'

'He died here—in Vienna?' Baroness Feldbach responded. 'How extremely sad—and what a shock for you! You were not with him, then?'

'It was near Marienwald, in fact. No, I was not with him, and it was a great shock. I came here principally to see his grave.'

'Did he know our family well? I am afraid I cannot recall ever having met him.'

'It was a long time ago—and as far as I know, he was more acquainted with the Phönix family than the Feldbach.'

I was handed a cup of tea and the choice of cream cakes. Adèle spoke for the first time, her voice rather tight and strained.

'Then—perhaps—he knew my mother?'

'I believe he did, though he never spoke to me of her.'

'I wish he had. It seems such a long time since she died.'

'Now, my dear, do not distress yourself. It will not do you any good,' said her stepmother.

'You are not well,' I said to Adèle. 'I hope the trouble is not serious.'

She shifted restlessly on her couch. 'The doctor does not seem to know. I have lost my appetite, and that has weakened me.'

She did not look at me as she spoke, as if to imply, I thought, 'you need not believe this'.

'My dear, you really must make an effort! The cook does her best to make the food attractive to you.'

Adèle did not answer, but sipped her tea. I noticed she had refused a cake. Then, 'Dr Haas is a fool!' she said.

'Oh, Adèle, he has had years of experience, and is considered very knowledgeable.'

'He is practically doddering.'

The Baroness's doll-like face showed a flash of annoyance, but it went as soon as it came, and she answered smoothly, 'If you think that, my dear, we will find you another doctor.'

'Oh, don't bother—it won't make any difference.'

I felt sure she was trying to tell me something in an oblique way. There was an awkward silence while I frantically tried to think of something to say. I did not want either of them to enquire further into my father's acquaintance with their family, for I could tell them nothing. The fact that I suspected he had once been in love with Adèle's mother was hardly a tactful matter to mention.

'How suddenly the weather has changed,' I said. 'I have actually been skating—at the Skaters' Palace. It was quite delightful.'

We began to talk about skating—that at least was a safe subject—when the door opened, and to my surprise the fair-haired officer in sky-blue who had been on the train with Count Palkany entered unannounced. He came swaggering over, and kissed both Baroness Feldbach and Adèle on the cheek. Baroness Feldbach put her arms up to him; Adèle was totally unresponsive. My mystification at his behaviour was ended when the Baroness introduced him.

'Lady Charlotte, may I present my son, Erich Szarvas? My son by my first husband, of course. Such a great fellow! You can tell how young I was!'

She gave a little lift of the shoulders and a pout.

'It hardly seems possible, Baroness,' I said as I gave him my hand, wondering why the name was familiar.

He looked at me with a certain guarded inquisitiveness, bowed, said a greeting and then turned to the girl. 'And how do you feel today, my dearest Adèle? I am longing for an improvement in your health.'

The affection, the sympathy, to me did not ring true.

'I am no better,' she said shortly.

'Erich, Adèle has no confidence in Dr Haas,' Baroness Feldbach said. 'Do you think we should call in another doctor?'

He turned from Adèle to her, and I could have sworn that beneath the look of concern—false concern—there was malice near to cruelty.

'Of course, Mama. I would advise you to get another opinion at once. Who knows, he might recommend some time in a sanatorium.'

Adèle said nothing, but I thought I saw a flash of fear in her eyes.

'Naturally we are all very concerned about Adèle's health,' Baroness Feldbach said to me. 'And Erich finds it most distressing. You see, it was intended that he and Adèle should marry.'

I was shaken. Of course, it was the old servant who had mentioned his name. But he was her stepbrother!

'I cannot marry until I am well,' said Adèle.

'Of course not, my dearest,' Szarvas responded. 'But soon we shall have only two options—either you are well, well enough to marry me, or you are so unfit that you must have special treatment. You cannot go on like this.'

His tone was very reasonable. I had no grounds to feel that his words carried a threat, but I did. Suddenly I was depressed, sick at heart. I seemed to see Adèle caught in the meshes of a great spider's web, and I could think of no way of releasing her. With cowardly relief I realised that my visit had been long enough for convention, and I began to take my leave. I thanked my hostess, said a formal goodbye to Szarvas, and moved over to Adèle.

Taking her hand, I said, 'It has been a great pleasure to meet you. I hope you will let me call again before I leave.'

'Oh, please—please do.'

Again there was that sudden tightening of the fingers, the frantic appeal in the look she gave me.

'Then you must improve, my dear,' said Baroness Feldbach. 'If you get any weaker, you will not be able to have visitors.'

That, too, sounded like a threat.

It was foolish of me, but I was thankful to get out into the open air and breathe its cold, crisp freedom. But before I did so, I managed a swift word with Gottlieb, giving him my address on a scrap of paper.

Having seen the young Baroness, I found that my feelings had changed. The matter had become personal. She was certainly in trouble, and I felt sure that had my father been alive his sense of chivalry alone would have been enough to make him do his utmost to help her. But what could *I* do?

I was not used to feeling incompetent, and it angered me. 'A lot of use you are, Charlotte Brantham!' I said to myself. 'Why, you haven't even sorted out the facts of Papa's death.' But, in my thoughts, I continued to argue that that wasn't quite my fault—I had tried to go to Marienwald again. And then it occurred to me that I might not need to go to Marienwald. It might well be enough to go to Baden. A little village like Marienwald would not have much in the way of resident authority. An accidental death would almost certainly have to be reported to Baden, and the relevant reports would be kept there. And Baden was accessible—if not by carriage, then by train.

I saw Captain Talbot that evening, and choosing my moment, broached the subject to him. 'I really must go to Baden,' I said.

'Baden, is it? And why?'

'I must see the police—or—or some authority there. The fact is—I know how my father died.'

I had decided I might as well take the bull by the horns, and see what the result might be. For a moment he said nothing, but gave me a clear, shrewd look.

'Yes. I told you.'

'And so did others. But I now know it was not typhoid fever. My father was shot.'

'And who told you that?'

'The priest. He said it was a hunting accident.'

'And you believed him? He is old, nearly senile. He must have been mistaken, and confused one death with another.'

'Why should he? He is old, but not senile. He would remember a stranger—an Englishman. He knows, because he saw . . . the body. The priest was quite definite—my father had been shot. So there is no need, Captain, to give me any more tales of typhoid and a kindly nurse.'

We sat in silence for several seconds.

'And if what the priest told you should be true, what do you expect to get from visiting Baden?'

'I expect someone in authority there to give me some detail.'

'What details?'

'I expect to be told exactly how such a thing could happen, where and when it occurred, and who was responsible.'

His face was set as he gazed at me; it told me nothing. At last he said, 'Lady Charlotte, you would be much better advised to leave the matter where it is. I admit you were told a tale, and I was made a party to it. But it was in your own best interests. The authorities wished to spare you distress as far as possible. But the matter has been investigated, judged to be an accident, and the case has been closed.'

'Then I think it was extremely high-handed!' I flared. 'To do all that without informing the victim's nearest relative! I consider my rights have been totally disregarded! You could at the very least have notified my father's lawyer.'

'Not I, Lady Charlotte. I am only a humble

Assistant Military Attaché. I do as I am told.'

'And I suppose you were told to escort me to Marienwald and prevent me from finding out the truth?'

'I was told to escort you and to look after your best interests.'

'Very well. It is now in my best interests to be told the truth, *in full*. You may, if you wish, take me to the officials in Baden who know that. If you do not wish to do so, I shall go by myself, and find out who they are. I do not care how long it takes me.'

'You are an unusually determined young lady. It would serve you right if I left you to fend for yourself! But I suppose there is no point in making things difficult for you.'

'None at all, unless it gives you pleasure.'

'I have more normal ways of amusing myself. I am not a sadist.'

'I am relieved to hear it.'

The rest of the evening passed in a state of antagonism and mutual distrust—a sad change after the pleasant times we had recently spent together.

Captain Talbot had said he could not manage to make the visit for a few days, and I had to believe him. But I could not help suspecting that in those few days he might arrange for my enquiries to be obstructed, or the reports doctored to tell me what the Embassy or the Austrian authorities wanted me to be told. However, the delay served me well in one respect, because two days after my visit to the Phoenix Palace, a note was delivered by hand for me.

The footman looked disapproving as he offered me on a silver salver a very cheap-looking and none too clean envelope. When I opened it, I found the message inside was brief:

> They have taken her away, we do not know where. They have all gone. The Palace is empty.

It was not signed, but I knew it came from Gottlieb's wife. It could refer only to Adèle. The phrase rang and echoed in my head, 'They have taken her away'. Of itself, that might cause no worry, but to me, as to the old servants, the fact that Adèle's whereabouts were now a secret seemed infinitely sinister. I racked my brains to find out what the servants had been unable to do, and found none.

It was then that I had the most extraordinary piece of luck. At one of our little tea-parties, a charming Viennese friend of Lady Bellanger, a delightful, bubbling, gossipy lady, had invited us to an informal soirée.

"I expect it will be quite a crush,' Lady Bellanger had said, and when we arrived, I saw that she was right. The rooms were crowded, and everyone seemed to be talking, laughing, drinking wine and nibbling tit-bits practically simultaneously.

I was introduced to a number of people I had not previously met, and then my hostess said, 'Lady Charlotte, you must meet Count Plesch. He is quite charming, and loves talking to English people.'

She half-hid her face behind her fan, and continued confidentially, 'Between ourselves, I am not so enamoured of his wife. She is . . . not quite . . .

you know . . . but we all tolerate her for his sake. She is his second wife, and he's far too besotted to see through her. She is having a raging *affaire* with young Szarvas, and her husband is the only one who doesn't know. He was a great catch for her —she ought to treat him better.'

Szarvas—who wanted to marry Adèle? Surely she was wrong?

'I have seen, but not met, a Countess Plesch —could it be the same one?'

'There is only one,' she said significantly. 'Over there.'

I followed her eyes, and nodded. Befrilled and bejewelled, it was the same Countess Plesch.

'Come and meet the Count.'

He was an elderly gentleman, with grey hair and whiskers and a solid, friendly face. He bore some resemblance to the Emperor Franz Josef, but looked so much more cheerful and informal. He tried to rise from his chair with the aid of two sticks.

'No, no, don't get up, Count,' said my hostess.

His eyes twinkled. 'Of course I must get up, when you, dear friend, arrive with a delightful young lady.'

We were introduced, he kissed my hand in a most courtly manner, and I sat down beside him. He said he knew England well and had a wide circle of English friends, but explained that nowadays he made few visits, as travelling was very difficult for him.

'Have you tried the Orient Express, Count?' I asked. 'It is amazingly comfortable.'

'So I hear,' he answered. 'My wife has not long

returned from Paris. She is trying to persuade me
. . . Ah, my dear!' He broke off to speak to someone behind me.

'Klärchen, here is a young lady who also speaks
well of the Orient Express.'

I turned to see Countess Plesch taking the chair
beside me.

She gave me a smile as hard and glittering as her
diamonds.

'We saw each other on the train, did we not?' she
remarked. 'What a small world it is!'

'Do you like Vienna under snow, Lady
Charlotte?' the Count asked.

'I like Vienna under any conditions, Count.'

'Well said, my dear! The snow could be expected, but it has still come without warning, and
will disorganise us a little, I fear.'

He turned to his wife. 'I suppose you will not go
to Baden tomorrow, my dear, as you planned?'

'Oh, I don't know. Not by carriage, of course,
but the trains will be running.'

'My wife is so good-hearted,' he said to me. 'She
will do anything for her friends. She has visited her
sick cousin in Paris, and now she is dashing to and
fro from Baden, helping a friend to get a sick
daughter settled at the spa.'

My heart beat faster. 'The waters are truly
beneficial, I believe,' I heard myself saying.

'Undoubtedly. It is time I went for another
course—but I am a Viennese, my dear young lady,
and I do not want to miss Christmas here—and not
only because Christmas sweetmeats taste better
than sulphur springs.' His eyes twinkled, then he
became serious, and turned to his wife. 'So we shall

not have Baroness Adèle's company at Christmas? Have you any news of how she is?'

'It is too soon to hear,' his wife answered coolly.

Baroness Adèle! Now my heart really was thumping.

'I suppose so. One hopes it is not the consumption.'

He turned back to me. 'Such a sweet girl; but lately, they say, she has lost all appetite and become quite wasted. Her stepmother was making plans for her to marry, and there is a young man waiting on the doorstep, you might say. But of course she must get well first, so everything is in abeyance. Young Szarvas must be so upset.'

I plied my fan, while my mind grappled with the situation. Remembering the trio on the train, I could believe in the possibility of a flirtation between Countess Plesch and Szarvas—but, a 'raging *affaire*'? When she was married, and he was trying to marry Adèle! Viennese life did seem to be complicated!

The Countess was tapping her foot, either in boredom or from impatience, I thought. The next moment, she caught a young man's eye and beckoned him over. He was quite the gallant, and in no time at all the Countess had manoeuvred us together, so I was drawn away from the old Count. It may not have been intentional, but for the rest of the evening I had no further chance to talk to him.

That night I lay awake in bed, thinking. So that is where Baroness Adèle is! They have taken her to Baden. And I had to admit that it did not sound at all sinister. She was ill; her stepmother was not pressing her to marry, but was trying to improve her health, and leaving the marriage question for the time being. The two old servants at the Palace had got the wrong impression. Perhaps they had some reason for disliking Countess Plesch, but she would hardly be urging a marriage with a young man with whom she herself was having an *affaire*, however much he wanted it for financial reasons. All the same, I could not reason myself out of worrying; I knew I would not rest until I had seen Adèle again. And since I had arranged to go to Baden, it would be an ideal opportunity to try to find her there.

Lady Bellanger was rather put out by my insistence on going to Baden. She was very busy with preparations for Christmas entertainment and did not want to give up a day to go with me, which I understood, but it still took a little while to convince her that as she had relaxed convention and allowed me to visit Marienwald with only Tilde for chaperon, she could well do the same for Baden. When she agreed, I thought it advisable not to tell her that I intended to stay for a night—that would be a sure way of being prevented from doing it at all.

The night before we were to leave, I packed a travelling-bag with what was absolutely necessary for an overnight stop. I could buy things in Baden, and if I had to live in one gown I was prepared to do so. Tilde, mercifully, had been trained to do as she was told without asking questions; she looked surprised at the orders I gave her in the morning, but obeyed them. She sent for a cab to come for her at the servants' entrance, and twenty minutes before Captain Talbot was due to call for me, she left with my travelling-bag to buy her own ticket and board the train.

The Captain arrived, not in uniform but in civilian clothes covered by his Chesterfield overcoat; though not so dashing as his scarlet and gold, it had an air of quiet distinction.

'Where is your maid?' he asked.

'Tilde has gone ahead. I thought she might as well get her ticket and find her place.'

His eyebrows lifted; he could not think I wanted to be alone with him, so was he wondering whether I suffered from some form of snobbery and did not wish to share a first-class compartment with my maid, or did he think it was a rich woman's parsimony? But he made no comment, and we said our goodbyes to Lady Bellanger and set off for the Southern Railway Terminal. There was no difficulty: in spite of the snow the trains were running fairly normally, and we were soon in a compartment alone. Not many people were travelling—in this cold weather it was something to be avoided. I noticed how English the Captain looked, tall and slim and elegant among the rather stocky figures in loden green.

After the Orient Express, I found the first-class compartment quite poor and uncomfortable, and was glad of the hand-warmer I had slipped inside my muff. Luckily it was not a long journey. At first the Captain and I talked little, for after our last meeting we were not on good terms, and I felt considerable restraint, for since then I had decided that I could not trust him. Ostensibly he was an escort; in fact, I was sure he was with me to put obstacles in my way. In addition, I was a little nervous about his reaction when I told him I intended to stay in Baden, but I pushed that to the back of my mind and sat looking out of the window at the snow-covered slopes and the mountains where the white was broken patchily by the dark green of firs.

I had the feeling that while I was looking out of the window, he was sometimes looking at me. When I caught his eye, he was wearing that set expression I had seen before, which told me nothing and was rather intimidating. We chugged along for some time, but then the Captain broke the silence and began to talk about Vienna. He did not paint the picture I expected.

'You have seen only the good face of the city,' he said. 'There is a lot of poverty and unemployment among the lower classes. This Christmas there will be many hard pushed to get enough to eat. They have plenty of courage, they will celebrate somehow, but it will only be by scraping and contriving.'

'I suppose that is true in all big cities,' I said soberly.

'Yes. But here the atmosphere is different. The poverty is, of course, on one level. On the other you have the comfortable bourgeoisie, the moneyed people, and the aristocrats. You would think *they* hadn't a care in the world. Everywhere they insist that Vienna is gay, with a light-heartedness you find nowhere else. At the balls —you haven't been to a ball, have you?—everyone dances to the Strauss waltzes, drinks champagne and flirts madly . . . It seems utterly delightful. But gradually you get the feeling that it is all happening inside a great crystal globe, and everyone knows that at any moment the glass may shatter and let reality in.'

I stared at him in silence. It was such a strange speech.

'You don't believe me?' he said. 'Did you know the suicide rate here is higher than in any other European capital? And it is not just the poor people who end their lives, the proportion is higher in the middle classes, and in case after case you would say that the people, and they are often young people, have everything to live for.'

I shivered. 'Why are you telling me this?'

'I don't quite know. Perhaps I want you to realise that what appears on the surface can be deceptive. Because nothing has changed for so long here, I believe a kind of desperation has set in. Nothing is as stable as it seems. People who poke around too much sometimes find the ice cracking beneath them.'

'Do you mean . . . Are you warning me not to press my enquiries?'

'No. But there is a relevance. If you find Austrian bureaucracy obstructive, it may be as well to accept it. I do not press matters myself, for I know it to be useless. And, as you see, in order not to cause antagonism I am not wearing uniform. Remember we are going to request, not to demand, information.'

'I am prepared to accept what you say about Austrian bureaucracy. But the rest—the suicides, the unreality—I find that incredible.'

He shrugged. 'The suicides are fact. You have only to read the newspapers to see them. As for the rest, Vienna is like a beautiful juicy peach—fully ripe, overripe—beginning to rot. In other words, this delightful society is degenerating, almost without knowing it.'

I found the conversation quite disturbing, and was glad when we pulled into the station at Baden. We stood on the platform for a few moments looking for Tilde, then we both saw her coming towards us with my bag clutched in her strong peasant's hand.

'What on earth has she got there?' said the Captain.

'It is my bag. Could you recommend me a good hotel, Captain? I should like to book in, and leave Tilde there.'

His brows drew together. He looked cross and incredulous at the same time—quite an achievement.

'*A hotel!* You do not intend to *stay*?'

'Indeed I do. You should be grateful—you will be spared my company on your return journey.'

'My good woman!' he exploded. 'You do not think I can leave you here—alone!'

'I see nothing against it.'

'Well, *I do*! It is simply not done for a young —lady—to stay in an hotel unaccompanied.'

'Surely it would be worse if you came too?' I said sweetly. I could not resist it—especially after being called his 'good woman'.

'Heaven help me!' he burst out.

Tilde had by now reached us and was watching our incomprehensible exchange with great interest.

'Do you not realise you would be putting your reputation at risk?' he thundered. 'And not only your reputation!'

'Please go on.'

'There's nothing more to say! You cannot stay here alone.'

'I think the man is waiting to take our tickets. The platform is empty.'

I played my trump card. 'Tell me, Captain. If it is quite all right for the Empress Elizabeth to travel all over Europe, and frequently to go off on expeditions quite alone, in the mountains or wherever she fancies, why cannot I stay alone in a civilised small town at a respectable hotel?'

'Because—because she is the Empress and a married woman, and you are—an unmarried, flighty, irresponsible, pig-headed little hussy who ought to be spanked!'

This was splendid—I had really rattled the self-possessed, irritatingly competent Captain! As we moved out of the station, I replied, 'I accept that I am unmarried and pig-headed—though I would have preferred "obstinate". But I do not consider I am flighty or irresponsible, and I am not sure about the "hussy". No, I have thought this over very carefully, and consider I may not finish what I want to do in one day. In addition, I wish to spend a little while—perhaps a week—taking the waters.'

He opened his mouth, and shut it again—snap! —as if what he wanted to say was not fit to pass his lips and reach my ears. We moved towards the cab-rank.

'Very well,' he said. '*One night*—since I imagine the alternative would be to drag you shrieking to the train, which would do neither of our reputations any good and would probably land me in a police cell.'

The thought of it made me want to giggle, but I stifled that and also the smirk of triumph which was threatening to creep over my face. The Captain gave the cabbie an address, which turned out to be that of a moderate-sized hotel, rather old-fashioned, very comfortable, and of course eminently respectable. The furnishings of the foyer, 'rich, not gaudy', I thought, spoke of utter propriety, while the hall porter and the reception clerk oozed respectability at every pore.

I was able to book two adjoining rooms for myself and Tilde.

'Unfortunately, Lady Charlotte is obliged to stay alone except for her maid until other arrangements are settled,' Captain Talbot remarked.

'Quite so, sir.'

I caught the clerk giving a covert glance at my hands. I had just signed the register, and knew what he was looking for. He could not tell from my signature whether I was married or not. But my left hand was still gloved. His attitude to Captain Talbot gave me the impression he was ready to accept the Captain as my fiancé—an assumption which would be as unwelcome to him as to me, I was pleased to consider.

I said a few parting words to Tilde, and then the Captain practically hustled me outside. He gave me a stiff arm and positively marched me down the street for a short distance, then turned into a tempting-looking coffee-shop.

Silently we seated ourselves at a corner table.

'Coffee?' he barked at me.

'A *mélange*, please'—that was topped with whipped cream—'and . . .'

'And a cream cake, I suppose?'

'That would be delightful.' I had totally succumbed to the cream cakes in Vienna.

'You will have yourself to blame if you get fat and lose your figure.'

'That is the second time you have mentioned my figure! Really, Captain Talbot!'

He leaned towards me over the table. 'There are other things I would like to mention. Such as how insufferable you are, and yet how . . .'

The waiter appeared for our order. He broke off, and when the man had left, I waited.

'And yet how . . . ?' I said.

'I have forgotten.'

'Don't think better of it, Captain. Be as rude as you like.'

'I was going to say, how utterly charming and lovely. Any man who marries you will have all my sympathy.'

'Are your compliments always so two-edged? Well, I do not think I shall marry. I prefer to keep my independence, and to plague people like you. Oh, what beautiful cakes!'

Suddenly he laughed. It was so genuine and unexpected that I, too, had to laugh.

'How can I go on being furious with you when at the sight of a plate of pastries you turn into a ten-year-old! Let us declare a truce.'

'A truce,' I agreed.

But there would be more battles to come, that was certain.

CHAPTER FIVE

I WAS GLAD we had had the coffee and cakes before we went to the Police Headquarters, as it was soon obvious that we were going to be there a long time. Captain Talbot stated our business, and then we sat and waited. One police officer went to another; he disappeared into an inner office; he came out again, and still we waited. There is no point in going into details: we were passed from hand to hand, from office to office, until eventually we were ushered into a Presence—some kind of Superintendent, I believe—who was treated as if he were, and obviously considered himself to be, little lower than the Emperor himself.

The interview, mainly conducted through Captain Talbot, as though I understood no German and was a half-wit into the bargain, was formal, stiff and punctilious in the extreme, until I began to lose patience. The death had been fully investigated, he insisted, and was judged to be a hunting accident. The evidence was satisfactory.

'I should like some details,' I said, as deferentially as I could.

'Details? What details?'

'Where it happened—why it happened—who was responsible—what was the evidence . . . ?'

He looked down his nose in disapproval that I should ask anything. 'It happened on the Palkany estate.'

I stiffened with shock.

'Who can say *why* it happened?' he went on. 'Some of these young gentlemen are impetuous, they fire at a movement, when they know there should be no hunters or beaters in the area. It was impossible to say who was responsible.'

'*Impossible?* Yet you have evidence.'

At my incredulity, he stiffened even more.

'Yes. The young gentlemen have said there was quite a lot of indiscriminate firing. They took collective responsibility. They were extremely shocked that such a thing could occur to a guest.'

'*A guest?*'

I was even more shaken. Papa a guest of Count Palkany? And he had been pretending total ignorance!

'Naturally, *gnädiges Fräulein*. How else would milord be there? He was one of the hunting party.'

I gathered my scattered wits together. 'In that case, why did not his host get in touch with me?'

The Superintendent shuffled his papers and his feet. He, too, was losing patience; he thought the interview had lasted long enough.

'I doubt if he even knew of your existence. He had only recently met your father. He behaved perfectly correctly: he informed the police and the British Embassy at once. Naturally he expected the Embassy to get in touch with you.'

'*Correctly!* You shoot a guest and then do not even trouble to send a letter of regret to his relations! In England, that would be considered barbarous!'

'Lady Charlotte!'

The Captain's hand was on my arm, he was trying to stop me from saying more. The Superintendent took this opportunity.

'I think you will find that your Embassy handled the matter from that point. As far as the Austrian authorities are concerned, the matter is closed. No purpose can be served by prolonging this interview. I can but offer you my respects and deepest sympathy.'

He stood up and bowed. 'Good day.'

I was dismissed. I was amazed, and so baffled that I did not know what else to say. I actually accepted his farewell, returned it, and let the Captain lead me from the room. We had walked through all the corridors and were out in the street before I recovered my powers of speech.

'It's incredible!' I said. 'It's monstrous! I have actually met Palkany, and he pretended to know nothing! He even tried to flirt with me!'

'It is typical,' the Captain said. 'He is one of the aristocratic gilded youth. I dare say he requested the Embassy to handle you as tactfully as possible and washed his hands of the matter. The Embassy tried to spare you distress. But you were not as easily satisfied as most young ladies would have been, and have caused yourself precisely the kind of heartache we tried to avoid for you.'

'Oh, I see! It is my fault again! You all thought you could feed me with lies, and I'd take them —like spooning food into a baby! If I could, I'd—I'd spit it back into your face!' How I could be so vulgar I don't know, but that is what I said.

The Captain was quite unruffled. 'You are doing that very successfully, Lady Charlotte,' He steered

me round a corner. 'Now we will get nothing more
out of the police. Let us go and have luncheon.'

'*Luncheon!* I couldn't eat a crumb!'

But when I was in a warm, cosy restaurant,
sitting on a red plush banquette, with one waiter
shaking out my napkin and another proffering a
large menu, I decided that my sinking stomach and
my miserable thoughts needed the solace of food.

'Well, I shan't improve matters by starving,' I
said.

'Very sensible,' replied the Captain. 'Let us find
out what the head waiter recommends.'

The warmth, the good food and wine lulled my
brain into acceptance until we reached the coffee
stage. Then it began to make a little protest.

'I wonder,' I said thoughtfully, 'what my father
was doing, hunting with those people. He liked to
know the sorts of shots he was with. And he was
very experienced—I can't think how he could get
into the line of fire.'

'I presume he met them socially, and accepted a
chance invitation. The Superintendent said they
admitted to quite a lot of indiscriminate firing.
Your father was very unfortunate, but such things
do happen.'

'I suppose so.'

I might have said more, but for once I had the
sense to hold my tongue. Palkany was involved in
the plot to make Adèle marry Szarvas, and I was
determined to find Adèle. If I let my tongue run
away with me, I might betray my interest in that
matter. If Captain Talbot knew I was interfering in
a purely Viennese matter, he might be even more
obstructive.

The Captain left me in the late afternoon. I dined alone in the hotel, visualising him taking the Vienna train and going to the Embassy to report. It was rather dull having no Captain with whom to cross swords over the dinner table, and I went to bed early.

For once, I had no plans. I wanted to find out more about Palkany, and to search for the Baroness Adèle, and could not think how to do either. I received no inspiration overnight. I woke in good time, and was sufficiently tired of my own company and my frustrating thoughts to go down to breakfast in the dining-room where I could at least see other people. I made breakfast last as long as I could. When I walked out into the foyer, a tall man unfolded himself from a chair and came towards me. It was Captain Talbot.

'Good morning, Lady Charlotte. Do not look so surprised. May I talk to you for a few minutes?'

'What are you doing here? Where have you been?' I demanded.

'As you implied yesterday, it would not have been proper for me to stay in the same hotel. There is another excellent place a couple of hundred yards down the road.'

'But you . . .'

'I take my duties seriously.' His face was unsmiling, but I thought I caught a twinkle in his eye. He had stolen a march on me: I felt positively outflanked. 'But I cannot stay in Baden indefinitely, as I am supposed to be at the Embassy. Equally I cannot leave you here, alone in a hotel and without an escort. I have thought of an alternative.'

Had he, indeed!

'I have acquaintances here—a charming young married couple. I visited them yesterday evening. They would like to meet you, and to offer you the hospitality of their house.'

'I can't possibly inflict myself on perfect strangers!'

'You will not be a stranger to Mitzi Krems for more than thirty seconds, I assure you! She loves company and will enjoy taking you about. She speaks fractured English, through which she will teach you to talk like a Viennese.'

I considered this. It sounded much more enjoyable than staying in the hotel, and it was likely that this Mitzi might be able to help me to find the Baroness.

'That is very kind,' I said. 'I should like to meet her.'

We drove about Baden for a little while, with the Captain pointing out places of interest along the snowy streets, and then took coffee to spend some more time; for Mitzi, the Captain said, was not an early riser. When we reached the house, the hostess, in an elegant *peignoire*, greeted the Captain with every sign of pleasure.

'Piers!' she trilled. 'Tell me you have changed your mind and will stay in Baden for a few days?'

'No, Mitzi, I really cannot. May I present Lady Charlotte Brantham? Lady Charlotte—Frau Mitzi Krems.'

'Just Mitzi, please! Anything more makes me feel so *old*! So, Lady Charlotte, *you* will stay? You will so much brighten my dull existence.'

'If you are to be Mitzi, I must be Charlotte—I should like that. And I should love to stay a few days. It is so kind of you to take in a complete stranger.'

'No! You are a friend of Piers, so you are not a stranger! But it is most provoking of him to run away at once. I am sure that wretched Embassy can get on very well without him.'

'I am sure it can,' replied the Captain blandly. 'Still, I have to be there.'

We chatted together for a little while and then the Captain took his leave, kissing Frau Krems's hand and bowing to me. I cannot think why I was piqued—he was treating me English fashion; besides, in France, it was not customary to kiss the hand of an unmarried girl; perhaps it was the same in Austria. Nevertheless it would have been a novel experience to have my hand kissed by Captain Talbot. And disappointingly dull, in all probability, I told myself.

Mitzi and I got on famously. She was what I needed, someone to distract me from thoughts of the criminal carelessness, the brutality, surrounding my father's death. Mitzi was no intellectual; it would have been hopeless to attempt a serious discussion with her, but her wit was like quicksilver and though she appeared superficial, she had a heart as big and warm as a feather-bed. She was small, dark, plump, with large brown eyes and a fascinating smile which usually developed into a throaty, gurgling laugh, distinctive and irresistible.

'Have you known Piers long?' she asked.

'No—a very short while.'

'Oh! I have known him for *ages*—he knew my husband before we were married. We are so glad he is in Vienna, though *he* does not care for it.'

'Doesn't he?'

'Oh, no! He would much rather be fighting—men have such extraordinary tastes—or doing whatever soldiers do the rest of the time. You know he was wounded quite badly—somewhere in India, the frontier to the north-west, where the tribesmen are quite horrid—and was sent to England to recover?'

'I didn't know. So he—he isn't fit for active service?'

'Oh, he is *now*. But they like him at the Embassy here, and he hasn't managed to get back to his regiment yet.'

It was not Mitzi's English that was fractured as much as her accent; the Captain had done her less than justice. She talked to me in a mixture of English and Austrian—I dared not say German, for the accent was so different. I tried to speak to her in German, and was rewarded with peals of laughter.

'Oh, forgive me, Charlotte! You speak German very well—but this is not Berlin. I am sure you have been excellently taught, but to me it is like talking to an old German professor! It really does not suit you—you are so young and charming!'

The last remark softened the blow considerably, and I remembered what the Captain had said.

'Then won't you teach me to talk like a Viennese?'

'That would be great fun! *Himmel!* Look at the time—I must dress for luncheon. We must see if your maid has come with your luggage.'

At the right moment I made an excuse for my limited baggage, and said I hoped we could go shopping together. As I expected, Mitzi thought that a splendid idea. We went out that afternoon before the light failed, made some purchases, and Mitzi then decided we needed refreshment.

'Coffee and cream cakes?' I suggested.

'Oh, Charlotte!' She looked at me doubtfully. 'You have not even started to take the waters yet.'

'There's no hurry for that.'

When we were seated in the coffee-shop, she shook her head at me reprovingly. 'Remember your doctor's orders. Piers told me that you were here to have a course of the waters, and as you cannot stay long you must be thorough—at least four glasses a day. Also that you should not have cream cakes.'

'Not have . . . !' His cunning nearly left me speechless. The fiend!

'But he has never met my doctor!' (Neither had I, for a long time.) 'Exactly what did he tell you?'

'Let me think. Just what I said about the waters, and then—oh, "She has been advised not to indulge in cream cakes." That was it.'

I knew who had advised me! The man was a devil!

'I think you misunderstood him,' I said firmly. 'Having one cream cake is not *indulging*—he means I must not eat several at one time.'

'Oh, that is not so bad. And here they are! But I promised him I would see that you took the waters.'

I could not get out of that—after all, it had been my excuse to the Captain for staying. He knew what he was doing; he certainly won that trick! The waters tasted foul and reeked of sulphur, and dear Mitzi would sit and watch solicitously while I downed a glass, four times a day. I cannot imagine what good she thought they were doing me; I felt as though I were being poisoned.

Still, apart from the waters, it was pleasant. What we would call the Pump Room was not dissimilar to one in an English spa, a kind of hall with a fountain, and a counter where one collected glasses of water, little tables and chairs, and, thank heaven, the service included the availability of coffee and other refreshments which were most welcome to take away the taste of the hellish brew. It was comfortable and warm, and there was usually a quartet of musicians playing light Viennese music who trilled away in the background, while I sat and listened to Mitzi talking about the people.

She knew everybody. She knew them not only by name, she knew all about their private lives as well. I soon realised that not much was really private in Vienna or Baden. Mitzi was full of scandalous tales, which she retailed so amusingly that it was very difficult to be shocked.

Captain Piers Talbot thought he had spiked my guns by finding me a hostess who would make sure I took the waters and would not leave me to my own devices for long. In fact, he could not have served me better. If anyone knew the whereabouts of the Baroness Adèle, and what sort of man Palkany was, Mitzi would. All I had to do was to steer the conversation tactfully in the right direction, and let her talk.

It was not as easy as I thought it would be. Since I did not know anybody, I could not bluntly say, 'What do you know about so-and-so?', without arousing her curiosity. Again, since she knew everyone, we were seldom alone for more than two minutes; someone was always stopping to chat with us. It was not until the third day that the moment came.

I was struggling with my second glass of spa water when I glanced up and saw, coming through the door to the Pump Room, none other than the Countess Plesch, and just behind her the Baroness Elsa Feldbach. I took my opportunity.

'Why!' I exclaimed. 'Surely that is the Countess Plesch?'

Mitzi gave a quick look. 'You know her, then? And Baroness Feldbach who is with her?' What luck! I thought. It could hardly be better.

'I have met them both, but I don't know them at all.'

'Meet one, you meet both! They are as thick as robbers—no, thieves—and that silly woman will do anything the Countess asks.'

'Isn't she the stepmother of the Baroness Adèle Phönix?'

'That's right. You know *her*, then?'

'I have met her once. A long time ago my father knew a member of her family. I was hoping to see her again while I was here.'

'In Baden? Is she here? Well, I suppose she must be, for it's said her stepmother never lets her out of her sight—yet I haven't seen her.'

'I was told that she is in hospital, but I don't know where.'

'Ah, that could be it. I have heard rumours that she has been ill.'

'Do you know what is wrong?'

'Does anyone know? Some say the consumption,

some say she had fever, and some say it is a pretence, to spite her stepmother.'

'Why should she do that?'

Mitzi gave a gurgling chuckle. 'And why not? That wretched woman! It's said she wanted Adèle to marry her son.'

'Her son?'

'Oh, they are not related. *She* is Adèle's father's second wife—he's dead now—and her son is from her first husband. But it really would be too provoking for Adèle. The marriage would simply be intended to give young Szarvas control of her money, which he would immediately spend on horses, gambling, politics and Countess Plesch.'

'You really think her stepmother would try to press such a marriage?'

'It would not surprise me.'

The two women, I was relieved to see, had not come to drink the waters. They went to the other side of the Pump Room where coffee and refreshments were served. Mitzi had told me this was a favourite meeting-place.

'I must admit I had heard that the Countess was very friendly with a certain Szarvas. But surely it is not the same one?' I said, dangling more bait for Mitzi.

'Yes, of course! I told you so—the Baroness's son!'

'What! And the Countess wouldn't mind him marrying Baroness Adèle?'

Mitzi giggled at my naïveté. 'She is married herself! It is really a shame for her to cuckold that nice old Count for that worthless boy. No, I'm sure she would like him to marry money, for he has none himself, and she would see that some of it came her way. She is very fond of jewellery, you know.'

'I have noticed.'

'There!' Mitzi exclaimed triumphantly. 'He has arrived! With Count Palkany. Now watch. They will stroll around, greeting people, and then, quite by chance, they will pass the Countess's table. They will be surprised to see each other—and will join forces.'

Mitzi knew exactly how the conventions were satisfied. As she predicted, the two officers strolled along, bowing here, kissing a hand there, exchanging a few words of conversation, until they reached the table where the two ladies sat. Surprise was registered on both sides, the invitation made, and the two men sat at the ladies' table.

'It's like a play!' Mitzi giggled. 'Such good acting! And just look at Baroness Feldbach—how she dotes on that man!'

'Her son?'

'Oh, no! Well, yes, him, of course, but I meant Palkany. He completes a fine quartet. He is a rascal, and she is quite besotted with him. Personally, I would not care to be in love with Palkany!'

'No?'

'To be one of many women! And he does not care a straw for any of them. He is quite heartless, quite unscrupulous. I think he is a dangerous man.'

Around me I still heard the clatter of teacups, the clink of glasses, the sounds of laughter and conversation, the lilt of music; but diminishing everything, hammering in my head were Mitzi's words, so lightly spoken, 'a dangerous man'. They crystallised my impression of him, and I tried to sound offhand.

'Is he often here?'

'Quite often. They don't seem to spend much time with their regiments. They always hunt together here, you know—at Palkany's estate near Marienwald.'

A cold shiver ran down my back. My mind turned over Mitzi's last remark. I remembered that if Palkany and Szarvas had been hosts of a certain hunting party some months ago, they would know all about my father's death, and Palkany's questions to me when we had met in the street in Vienna had been a total pretence. Captain Talbot had said nothing to Mitzi about my father's death, though I saw no particular reason for his reticence. For a moment I considered telling her, then thought better of it.

'I suppose when he is not at his estate he lets other parties shoot there?' I asked.

'Good heavens, no! He is most particular to keep the shooting private. One guesses the place is a retreat for them, too; one doesn't ask what goes on there! It is, we suspect, not unlike the Crown Prince's lodge at Mayerling—a place to have visitors who cannot be received elsewhere.'

'You mean—*women*?'

I felt quite wicked even to talk about such things; in England they were never mentioned, though one knew they went on.

'Sometimes, but not always, in either case. It is said that the Crown Prince meets writers and other politically-minded people, because he is tired of being forced to be neutral, prevented from taking any part in government. As for Palkany, he is a Hungarian, and the Hungarians are always trying to make a fuss about something.'

I brought the conversation back to the subject which concerned me. 'Is it not rather odd that the four of them should sit there enjoying themselves if the Baroness Adèle is ill in hospital?'

'I suppose they know she is in good hands, and there is nothing they can do.'

'I wish I knew where she was. I should like to visit her.'

'Why don't you ask them?'

'No, I don't want to do that. I feel the Baroness doesn't like me—she would say I was interfering.'

'Would it matter? Well, I dare say I can find out for you.'

For the time being I left it at that, and hoped I had not been seen by the Countess's party. I should prefer them not to know I was in Baden.

Mitzi was as good as her word. She sent a man-servant to enquire at the hospitals—of which there were several in Baden—regarding the health of the Baroness Adèle. In two hours he was back, with the name of a private establishment that had the Baroness on its list of patients, and the information that her condition was satisfactory.

I could hardly contain my delight. I told Mitzi I should like to visit the Baroness that afternoon. She offered to accompany me, but I thought it better to go alone, so she put her carriage at my disposal.

The private hospital was not large, but it gave a very good impression. Plainly the building had originally been a mansion set in its own grounds on the outskirts of Baden. The gardens were beautifully kept even in this difficult season, and the gravel drives were clear of snow. When I alighted from the carriage, I saw that the steps to the main door were impeccably clean, the brass knocker, bell-pull and door handles gleaming like gold. I tried the door. It was locked. I tugged at the bell.

In a few moments the door was opened by a spruce maid in uniform and a beribboned cap, who looked at me enquiringly.

'I have come to see the Baroness Adèle Phönix,' I said firmly.

'I am not sure, *gnädiges Fräulein* . . .' she began diffidently.

'I am Lady Charlotte Brantham,' I told her, as if the name should open all doors.

'Oh—m'lady—will you step inside, and I will enquire.'

The hall was impressive, with a great deal of dark polished wood. The maid indicated a chair to one side, and seeing me seated, went through a door on the right which apparently led to an office. I heard the sound of low voices, and then the maid returned with a nurse. She was middle-aged, severe, unwelcoming.

'Lady Charlotte Brant?' she asked. I didn't correct her. 'I am sorry, but the Baroness is not allowed visitors.'

'But how ill is she? Is it really serious? Is she in danger?'

'No. It is not critical. But she is weak, and must not be disturbed.'

I was not going to be fobbed off if I could help it.

A touch of the arrogant English aristocrat might help, I thought.

'I shall not disturb her. I have come all the way from England, and I do not expect to be turned away without even a sight of her. Kindly ask the doctor to see me.'

I prayed fervently that the doctor was having an afternoon off duty; I could see a slight look of uncertainty on the nurse's face.

'I am sorry, m'lady, the *Herr Doktor* is not available.'

'Not available! In that case, I feel you must exercise your own authority. I shall not stay more than a few minutes, but I really must see how the Baroness is. I shall take all responsibility—you may refer the doctor to me.'

As I guessed, the nurse was the type who would tyrannise her subordinates but would give in before a show of rank or authority.

'Then, I dare say, I might allow you the briefest of visits, on condition that you do not disturb her in any way.'

'Naturally I shall be most careful.'

My heart was pounding with excitement as she led me up a gleaming staircase and along a well-carpeted corridor to a room near the end. It disturbed me to notice that she had to open the door with a key which was in the lock—the patient was actually locked in! She stood aside for me to enter.

It was a pleasant room, well furnished, warm, the long window nicely curtained, comfortable chairs, rugs on the floor, flowers on a bedside table. I was vaguely aware of all this, but my eyes at once went to the bed, where, propped up by many pillows, sat

Adèle. She had been reading—an open book lay on the counterpane. As we entered, her head turned from where it rested on the pillow to look at us. Her face beneath the swath of dark hair was now extremely pale and very thin, the cheekbones stood out above two hollows, the dark eyes in shadowed sockets flashed a look of caution, almost of fear, then brightened with an expression of near-incredulity as she recognised me. Her long slim hands which should have been beautiful were bony, almost skeletal, as they clutched at the covers.

'A visitor for you, Baroness,' said the nurse.

I smiled, as reassuringly as I could, and turned back with a 'Thank you' to the nurse, which I hoped she would take as a polite dismissal. She did.

'I shall be outside,' she told me.

I waited till the door was closed, then went over to Adèle and took her hand.

'Tell me,' I said. 'What is going on? What can I do to help?'

She caught her breath and spoke at last, in a voice only just above a whisper. 'You found me! But there's nothing you can do. *He* might have —Lord Hilary . . .'

Suddenly her manner altered, became urgent, agitated. 'Why didn't he do anything? I told him— I told him everything . . .'

Mercifully she had not raised her voice, and I tried to soothe her. The nurse would be on the chair outside the door, and might well have her ear to the keyhole.

'He died too soon,' I said.

Yes, several years too soon. I took a chair and

placed it beside the bed. I sat down and took her hand in mine again.

'Don't worry. I'm here now. You must tell me what is wrong.'

'*He* knew! But now, it's gone so far—and as for me, I might as well die—there's no point in anything. But I won't marry Erich!'

'No one can make you marry him,' I said soothingly. 'And you mustn't talk about dying—you're not going to die.'

'I could!' She stared at me wildly. 'It might be for the best. I'm not eating, you know. At first—when they said I must marry him—I said I'd starve myself sooner, and stopped eating. I knew it would look bad, you see, if they tried to force the marriage when I was ill and weak. I am here now—to teach me, they say—and if I eat they will let me out. *To be married!* If I starve again, I shall be sent somewhere worse. Plesch and my stepmother, they give me no peace. Now I can't stand the sight of food, it makes me sick . . . and they try to force me . . .'

She shuddered. Then suddenly all the urgency went out of her voice, she leaned back on the pillows and turned her head away from me.

'There's nothing you can do.'

I pressed her hand. 'There is,' I said firmly. 'I can help you, if you will be brave and do your part.'

She shook her head slowly.

At that moment the door opened; it was the nurse, carrying a tray which held a bottle of wine and a glass. I was thankful she had come at a time when Adèle was quiet. The nurse spoke with a false brightness.

'This is for you, Baroness. It arrived a little while

ago, but the silly maid forgot to tell me until now.'

She placed the tray on the bedside table. 'Look, herc is the message.'

Adèle took the stiff folded paper, opened it and read it.

'Let me pour you some now.'

'No. First, bring another glass for Lady Charlotte.'

'It is for *you*, Baroness, to help your appetite.'

'Bring another glass!'

The nurse's mouth tightened, but she nodded and left. Adèle handed me the note.

'That is amusing!' she said with a twisted smile. 'Countess Plesch and my stepmother are against me, and they bully me to eat, for their own ends —but the old Count, he's nice, and he's concerned, so he sends me a bottle of the best wine from his own vineyards.'

The note, written in an old-fashioned spidery hand and signed by Count Plesch, was brief but charming, sending best wishes and hoping the wine would help restore her to health.

'You see!' I reassured her. 'People care about you. You won't be forced to do anything you don't want to do.'

'You don't know,' she said wearily. 'They've kept me shut up—I can never get away from them. They stop this, they stop that—they tell such tales to the doctors—they'll do *anything*. They want the money. My father left *her* enough to live on, so why should they have mine? And I *loathe* Erich!'

I heard a sound outside and shushed her into silence as the nurse came in with another wineglass.

'Just a few minutes more, m'lady,' she said. 'Then you must go.'

'I understand.'

She went out again, and Adèle clutched my hand.

'How did you get in? It's not a trick?'

'I was determined to see you, because of my father. You must trust me, Adèle.' I felt in my reticule and brought out the keepsake. 'You see, I have this.'

She gave a gasp of relief.

'*He* had that! It was clever of Marthe to send him the crest, because I'd tried to write to him, and to the lawyer, and *she'd* stopped the letters.'

'A lawyer? Why hasn't he helped you?'

'He doesn't know. They won't let me see him —they'll tell him some tale. But he won't give them the money. In my father's will, the lawyer manages the money until I'm twenty-five or marry. That's why they want me to marry Erich. He's detestable! And, besides, how insulting to propose him as my husband when everyone knows that the Plesch woman is his mistress. You can imagine what he'd do with my money!'

I knew I hadn't much time. I must think fast, reassure her and try to make some sort of plan. While I was thinking, I poured out a glass of wine for Adèle, and a little in the second glass for myself.

'Drink some wine,' I said, 'and listen to me. We must be quick, the nurse won't let me stay much longer.'

She took the glass and gazed at me over the brim as she sipped the pale golden wine.

'Somehow I must get you away from here—away

from your stepmother, so that you are a free agent.
Then you must go to your lawyer and tell him
everything. But it's going to be difficult with you as
weak as this. So you must start eating.'

She shook her head. 'I can't—it sickens me . . .'

I drank a little of the wine, telling myself I must
not get cross with her.

'I know, but you can conquer that. Tell yourself
it is to make you strong so that you can escape.
Before, you couldn't escape on your own. But now
you're not alone—you have me, outside, and I'll
make plans to get you away from them.'

'Will you?'

For the first time I saw the vestige of a smile on
the thin white face, and heard a trace of hope in the
voice.

'Will you really get me away?'

'Yes, I will. But you must help. You must get
strong enough to walk. You must start eating—
very light food at first, and very little—you will
keep it down if you tell yourself it's to have strength
to fight them. And as soon as you can, get on your
feet and practise walking.'

'And then—what? How can you . . . ?'

She was failing, doubting again.

'I will find a way. I am very determined.'

'*He* couldn't! He didn't come back. Your father
—why didn't he come back? Why did he send you?'

I drank some more wine. 'Adèle, you know he is
dead. He must have died soon after he saw you.'

'Dead! Yes, dead—and I killed him! I told him
. . . Oh, I shouldn't have done so—and now you
have come! *Why*?'

'Of course you didn't kill him! How could you?

He died in an accident. I came because I had seen your servant's letter, and I remembered it when I saw the keepsake.'

'Yes, he's dead—how dreadful—I thought he didn't care about me after all . . .'

Her eyes filled with tears.

'Adèle!' I said urgently. 'You mustn't cry. If the nurse thinks I've made you cry, she won't let me come back. Listen. I don't know how long it will be before I manage to see you again. I must wait until you are strong, and you must be ready for me when I come. Will you remember that?'

She nodded.

'Let's drink to that,' I said.

We both emptied our glasses as the nurse came bustling in.

'You must go now, m'lady.' She refilled Adèle's glass. 'I'm glad to see you've taken some wine, Baroness. It's so good for you.'

'Goodbye, Adèle.' I bent and kissed the thin cheek. 'Remember, you must try to get your strength back.'

She nodded and gave me a little smile, but her look was vague, so that I was not sure whether she understood me. As I left the room, she was still smiling and nodding. The nurse hurried me out, closing and locking the door behind me.

'Why do you lock the door, nurse?'

'It is the *Herr Doktor*'s orders,' she replied. 'When she first came here, the Baroness walked in her sleep. He is afraid she might do so again and fall down the stairs.'

'She does not look capable of walking now.'

'She will get stronger. It is a safety precaution.'

'I am glad to see she is having such good care,' I said hypocritically. I felt in my bag and pulled out a gold piece, which I slipped it into the nurse's hand. 'Please buy yourself a box of bonbons for your trouble. You have been most kind.'

'Thank you, m'lady.'

The maid closed the door behind me and I stood on the top step. Mitzi's carriage was waiting for me on the broad gravel drive. I breathed in the fresh cold air, and suddenly felt giddy.

Everything about me began to lurch to and fro; the sunlight, before so pale and thin, seemed intense and splintered with colours, the shadows of the shrubs held deep blues and purples; it was an extraordinary sensation; and I told myself that I'd been giddy before, but not like this. I was not at all sure how to go down the steps: walking seemed so dull, I felt I could put my hand on the balustrade and glide down without touching the ground. But that, I decided, would be showing off, I had better walk.

I started down the steps—where were they? —and saw Mitzi's coachman, who had been standing by the carriage, start towards me. He caught me by the arm, and as he looked at me his face was shifting as though I were seeing it reflected in moving water. His voice sounded very loud.

'*Fräulein!* You are ill!'

I shook my head. Of course I wasn't ill—I felt wonderful, but it wasn't easy to speak. He was helping me towards the carriage. There was a splintering, crashing noise. It was only another carriage coming up the drive. I tried to drag my thoughts together.

The coachman was speaking urgently, 'Had you better go back inside, *Fräulein*, and see the doctor?'

Making a great effort, I said, 'No . . . No, take me home.'

Somehow, with his help, I got into the carriage. We swept round the curve of the drive as the other one drew up. I felt better, safer, sitting down. I looked out as the other carriage stopped, and saw, as if in a distorting mirror, the face and figure of Countess Plesch.

I laughed. I clapped my hands. I swayed to and fro on the seat. I don't know if I spoke out loud or not, the words were thundering in my head, 'I was just in time! I was just in time!'

After that, I was only vaguely aware of things. I have an impression of floating out of the carriage, into the house, and upstairs; of voices around me saying phrases like—'The *gnädiges Fräulein* seems ill . . .' 'Charlotte, whatever is wrong?' 'We must get her to bed.'

Then Tilde was undressing me and Mitzi was watching me with a sad, anxious face. I could not think why. Everything, including Mitzi's face, was still shifting and distorting, but it didn't worry me. Nothing worried me.

'It's all right,' I managed to say. 'Bed—sleep —dreams—nothing wrong . . .'

'I shall send for the doctor.'

'No. No doctor—sleep . . .'

It was bliss to lie in bed. I do not know if I slept or not, for my head was full of fantastic visions, of thoughts which were staggering in their brilliance, their immensity. I must remember that—and that

—I am so clever, how surprised everyone will be
. . . Then I either slept or became unconscious, for
the next thing I remember is finding everything in
my bedroom dull and normal, of being unable to
remember a single one of my brilliant ideas, of
feeling very sad, of knowing that the world was a
miserable place, so miserable that one wondered
why people stayed in it.

Mitzi appeared, and then the maid with a bowl of
broth. I drank it to avoid arguments. I was too
depressed even to talk to Mitzi. I lay back, trying
not to weep, and slept again.

When I woke, it was morning, and Piers Talbot
was standing by my bed.

'What are you doing here?' I demanded.

'Mitzi telegraphed me. She said you were ill.'

I pulled myself together. 'I am perfectly well.
Oh—I have a headache . . .'

'I'm not surprised. Drunk, before six in the
evening!'

'I was not drunk!'

—Or was I? The dreadful realisation struck me
that I could have been. On a third of a glass of
wine? But it might have been very strong, and I
had also taken wine with my luncheon, and I was
used to drinking only a very little. I had no idea
what being drunk was like. So that was it. Oh,
how undignified this was, to be lying in bed
with Piers Talbot looking at me with a kind of
cynical amusement, positively gloating over my
downfall!

'Get out of my bedroom, Captain Talbot!'

'Now I know you have recovered! You are quite
your old self.'

He left, and I contemplated the possibility of getting up and dressing. Mercifully, Tilde appeared with coffee and croissants, and having taken them, I felt better. My headache was bearable, my legs functioned and my brain was clear enough to start asking questions. I got up, dressed, and joined Mitzi and Captain Talbot in the morning-room. Mitzi's husband, Schani, was out, and I was glad. He was very nice, but two people were as many as I could face.

'Charlotte, I don't want you to go, but Piers thinks it better that you should return with him,' Mitzi said to me.

He would. He is determined to keep an eye on me, I thought.

'But I am not ready to go back, as long as you don't mind me staying.'

'But, Lady Charlotte . . .' he interposed crisply.

'Captain Talbot!' I snapped back.

'*Himmel!* You two!' Mitzi cried. 'For heaven's sake, call each other Piers and Charlotte—then you can fight in a proper fashion!'

I had got so used to hearing Mitzi call him Piers that it seemed reasonable to me.

The Captain glared, then said, 'Well, are you as sick of the conventional address as I am—*Charlotte*?'

I remembered he had inadvertently called me that once before.

'Yes, *Piers*. It is a good idea to be on Christian-name terms with the enemy.'

'Very well. Now, Charlotte, I do not wish to exert my authority, but you, I believe, are under twenty-one, and I, at the moment, am in the position of guardian. I must insist that you return to Vienna with me.'

I knew from the set of his jaw that argument would be useless, but I had to make a show of resistance.

'And if I refuse, will you call an armed escort?'

'A good idea. No, I think I should call the police—the Baden police would be glad to see the back of you.'

'You wouldn't dare!'

'I wouldn't need to. I'd manage without. But I think you'll be sensible.'

I thought hard. 'I'll consider it. But before I go back to Vienna, I must pay another visit to my friend who is in hospital.'

'Then I shall take you there.'

He not only went in the carriage with me, he marched up the steps beside me and rang the bell himself. The same little maid opened the door, and her eyes widened with surprise when she saw me.

'I should like to see the Baroness Phönix again,' I said.

'Oh, *gnädiges Fräulein*, it's not possible!'

'You said that before,' I reminded her.

'But today . . .'

She was thrust aside by the nurse, who had appeared behind her. 'So it's you, m'lady!' she said. 'If you have been hoping to see the Baroness Adèle—you cannot. Visitors are absolutely forbidden.'

There was something antagonistic, almost vindictive, in her expression as she went on, 'She had a severe relapse last night. She will not be fit to see anyone for several weeks, and even when she is fit, you will not be allowed in.'

'But, nurse, she was so pleased to see me!'

The nurse's eyes narrowed. 'Was she, indeed? I suppose you have no idea what trouble you have caused? You excited her so much that you nearly sent her out of her mind! You will never be admitted here again. And you need not try to bribe me—you almost cost me my job!'

She closed the door in my face, and I just stood there, stunned.

'Come, Charlotte.' Piers was offering me his arm, and I took it.

There was nothing more I could do in Baden.

CHAPTER SIX

ON THE train journey back, I was very subdued. I
did not think Piers Talbot noticed it, for we did not
have the compartment to ourselves. Had we been
alone, I don't think I could have talked to him. I
was worried, confused, and intensely embarrassed.
That I should get drunk and cause Mitzi to telegraph for him! It was appalling, and I still could not
think how it had happened. I had been perfectly
normal on arrival at the hospital, and had drunk
very little of Adèle's wine.

Poor Adèle! What a wretched coincidence that
she should have had a relapse that very day. What
sort of relapse could it have been? With under-
nourishment, surely a person would simply weaken
until they fell into a coma— and there was the nurse
talking about Adèle being nearly out of her mind!
Could my visit really have excited her to that
extent? I found it hard to believe. But it certainly
looked as if I had done nothing but harm to an
already delicate situation.

So that was where my meddling had got me. I had
injured the person I wanted to help, and disgraced
myself into the bargain. I had satisfied my ridiculous curiosity, and found out what was going on
—and much good it had done me. I had done
nothing for Adèle, either. I knew now that her
stepmother was in love with Palkany, that she
wanted to marry Adèle to her son so that he could

have control of her money, and that her son was Countess Plesch's lover. It was a disgusting tangle. Piers's words came to mind—'a degenerating society'—yes, that was it. I no longer wanted any part of it. Then I remembered Adèle's pale face, and thought, She is the innocent one, she is suffering. It was strange how since meeting her I always thought of her as Adèle, never as the Baroness, and how, as soon as I had seen her, I had felt as if I knew her; more than that, as if we were somehow very close. How could I go away and leave her, especially as I was responsible for worsening her condition?

Yet there was nothing I could do. If I told Piers or Lady Bellanger what was going on, they would only half believe me, and would say we couldn't possibly interfere. I cursed myself for a fool—if only I had thought of it and made time to ask Adèle the name of her lawyer, I could go to him. He would have to do something. But without that name I was helpless.

It was selfish at such a time to be bothered about personal trivialities, but I was, so much so that when we were in a cab on the way from the Southern Railway Terminal to Lady Bellanger's house I broke my silence and asked the Captain a question.

'Is some of the Viennese wine very strong?'

He looked surprised, then suppressed a smile. Beastly man!

'It depends what you mean by very strong. It's not fortified, like sherry or port.'

'What is "fortified"?'

'Strengthened with spirit—usually brandy.'

'So a very good wine would not be much stronger than an ordinary table wine?'

'It would not have a much higher alcoholic content, no. Now, Charlotte, stop worrying. Everyone takes a little too much once in their lives. You enjoyed it—so just put it down to experience.'

By now I was blushing furiously, and knew it, but forgot my embarrassment because an idea had come to me which was frightening, which opened up dreadful possibilities, which I wanted to thrust from me but knew I must explore.

'Captain, will you tell me . . .' I started hesitantly.

'Piers, please.'

'Piers, then. Tell me—you must have some idea how much wine I could take without getting—tipsy —allowing for the fact that I am only used to drinking very little . . .'

'I could hazard a guess. But why don't you just forget the whole thing? As soon as Mitzi realised what it was, she wasn't bothered at all.'

'*I'm* bothered! Listen. I had luncheon, with one glass of red wine, nothing more, no liqueurs or brandy. It is better if you eat when you drink, isn't it? And I had a good meal. Later on I had some special wine, sent in to my friend in hospital, a very fine white wine—but I only had about a third of a glass—surely I shouldn't have been tipsy on that?'

He positively grinned at me. 'It depends on the size of the glass.'

'Don't be infuriating! It was a normal wine-glass. *You* are the one who said I was drunk. I don't believe I was.'

Now he was looking at me quite seriously.

'That was *all* you had? And you're sure it was wine, not spirit? Not a liqueur?'

'I'm not such a fool as that! It was wine.'

'That shouldn't have affected you. At the most you might have been a little cheerful, but certainly not the way Mitzi described you. But what is the alternative?'

Now I could look him in the eyes without being ashamed.

'Something I don't like to think about, but must. You heard the nurse say that Adèle had a relapse —that she was nearly out of her mind? We drank the same wine, but she had more than I did. I think the wine was drugged.'

'*Drugged?* That's pure fantasy! Where did it come from?'

'That's the awful thing. It was a special present, some of his own wine—from Count Plesch.'

'Plesch! Oh, no!'

'It's incredible, isn't it? Oh, Piers, I think I'll have to tell you everything.'

His face was grim.

'Yes, I think it's time I heard what you've been up to. But please don't think I'm going to believe any such nonsense as Count Plesch sending bottles of drugged wine to young ladies in hospital. My credulity will only stretch so far.'

'I've told you that I can't believe it myself, but . . . Oh, we had better wait until we get indoors.'

Once indoors and settled in the drawing-room —luckily Lady Bellanger was out—I began telling Piers my story. By now, suspicions were crowding on me thick and fast. I had come to distrust Palkany and Szarvas so much that I was beginning to wonder whether they had arranged my father's death, whether they were no better than murderers, but this was so tenuous that I thought I must leave it for the time being. Besides, it would be unwise to try, as he said, to stretch Piers's credulity, which was already strained to the uttermost. No, I must convince him of one thing at a time.

I showed Piers the medallion, told him of the appeal for help and my father's departure, and how after his death I had decided to try to follow the trail myself. I told him about my meeting with the old servants at the Palace, of their fears for Adèle, of my first meeting with her, of her removal, and of how I guessed from the conversation at the soirée that Adèle was in Baden. I tried to be brief, and as clear as possible. He sat with his eyes fixed on me, nodding at intervals. Then I told him in detail about my visit to the hospital, and how Adèle had confirmed the rumours and suspicions.

'So, you see,' I ended, 'those two women have every reason for trying to keep Adèle under their thumbs: they are both so greedy, they want her money for their own ends, and don't care what they do to get it. They'll have her drugged in order to dominate her.'

'I have followed your reasoning so far, but at this point we differ. The business of the wine makes no sense. How can you suggest that Count Plesch —that kind, honourable old man—could be involved in such a thing?'

'I am sure he wasn't—not consciously,' I answered. 'Now that I've thought about it, it's quite plain to me. He provided the wine, and the kind note, with the best of intentions. Travelling for him is difficult, and I know he does not intend to go to Baden before Christmas. But Countess Plesch goes

to and fro—of course she would take the wine
—and tamper with it before it was given to Adèle.'

He stared at me without speaking.

'It's possible, isn't it?' I pressed. 'I know nothing
about drugs, but there must be something almost
tasteless that could be used, and a way of getting it
into the wine without the bottle looking as if it had
been opened.'

'Yes,' he said slowly. 'I can see it's an attractive
theory to you. It fits with your suppositions.'

'They're not suppositions, they're facts! Adèle
herself told me, and . . .'

'But is she really reliable? Be sensible, Charlotte! A girl who can deliberately starve herself
must be pretty highly-strung—hysterical, one
might say. How do you know she isn't imagining a
lot of this? Her relatives might not be victimising
her at all, and she may be in hospital solely for her
own good. This relapse they speak of could have
been a fit of hysteria, which in her condition had a
very bad effect.'

'She is not hysterical! She is very weak, and being
constantly badgered and virtually imprisoned without any company is bound to have been bad for her.
She was in a state of despair—and why not? I told
you, she was locked in—*that* is not normal nursing.'

'There was a perfectly good explanation for
it.'

'It may satisfy you—it didn't satisfy me. And that
wine *was* drugged. The more I think of it, the more
sure I am. It had such a strange effect on me—and I
had only a little. Adèle had a glassful while I was
there, and probably more later. I'm not surprised
the doctor thought she was nearly out of her mind.

It's fiendish—they did not even know how much she would take—it's as if they didn't care what the effect on her might be.'

'If that's true, who are "they"?'

'Her stepmother and Countess Plesch, of course. You can also include Szarvas; he must be a party to it. I don't quite see how Palkany fits, though.'

'You'll get him in somehow! Didn't Mitzi say Baroness Elsa was besotted with him? You could consider he, too, could use some more money.'

'I think you're beginning to believe me.'

'I'm not sure. I feel that something is going on, but I can't believe it's as sinister as you say. I think it's possible she's a highly-strung, temperamental girl with an obstinate streak, and that her relatives are trying to do what is best for her *and* for themselves, and taking rather strong measures because she is unco-operative.'

'I might have known a man would find some way of glossing it all over! You haven't seen her—I have—and surely you don't call the drugged wine merely a "rather strong measure"?'

'I don't know, Charlotte. We don't *know* that it was drugged. I think we must both take time to consider it reasonably. In any case, there's nothing you can do at present. You've rushed one fence, and come a cropper. Don't go on looking for more trouble until you've got a clearer idea how the land lies.'

'But I can't get a clearer idea!'

'Then have a little patience. There's nothing you can do now,' he repeated. 'Charlotte, I want you to promise me you won't do anything without consulting me.'

'Well,' I said grudgingly, 'I won't for a few days.'

'That's no promise.'

'It's the best you'll get. Yes, I'll think about things.'

And with that he had to be satisfied. He was not, of course—but neither was I. The infuriating man with his logical arguments had raised a few doubts in my mind that I would have given a lot to be able to settle.

But I was not allowed to brood. Christmas was nearly on us, and Piers brought news of the Embassy Ball. He virtually insisted to Lady Bellanger that I should go, and 'For heaven's sake get her out of that mourning!' he added.

By implying that the mourning was entirely my choice, he made it easier for Lady Bellanger. She indicated to me that I could if I chose wear something light, and whether I was influenced by my recent depressing experiences or not I cannot say, but I jumped at the opportunity. Viennese seamstresses are quick and clever, and I was able to order a ball-gown to be made in time. In palest jade-green silk, it was to be overlaid and draped with matching net, embroidered with beads of crystal and pearl and trimmed with posies of imitation white Christmas roses. Being fashionable, it would be rather *décolleté*, and I was glad I had my pearl necklace and earrings with me.

Before the Ball, I was swept into the rush of Christmas preparations, and although I felt like a traitor to Adèle, I enjoyed it. But she was never quite out of my mind. How was she? I couldn't enquire. Better or worse, I wouldn't know. And one of Piers's remarks had disturbed me. 'Is she really reliable?' Time and again I thought back over our two meetings.

I had to admit that her manner when alone with me had not been consistent; one moment vehement, the next despairing. At first there was a time when I thought she had not been exclusively concerned with her own troubles; she had said of my father, 'I told him everything . . . he knew! But now, it's gone so far . . .' and then added, 'as for me, I might as well die . . .' And then I would change my mind, and decide she had been talking rather incoherently about her own situation, and that there could not possibly be anything else.

Then her reaction to the mention of my father's death was so strange; she had immediately burst out, 'and I killed him!' as though simply by telling him her troubles she had brought on his death. Piers could be right, she could be a hysterical girl being cared for in the best way her stepmother knew. It did not look as if I should be able to prove or disprove this. The conviction grew on me that the only effective action I could take would be to advise Adèle's lawyer of the situation—if I could only find out who he was. Then I thought, The servants at the Palace—they should know! I remembered their concern, and felt a prick of conscience that I had not told them I had traced their young mistress and that she was in hospital. I nearly rushed out to find a cab at that very moment, but Piers must have impressed me more than I knew, because I checked myself and waited to see him.

The day he came visiting, I was about to trim the

morning-room with fir branches, and he volun-
teered to help. He picked up an armful of branches
and carried them into the room for me, and I began
selecting what I wanted.

'Piers, I must go to the Palace and see the two old
servants again.'

He looked at me, cocking an eyebrow. 'Why?'

'Because they would like to know that I have
traced Adèle, and, besides, they might be able to
give me the name of her lawyer.'

'You want to go to him with the whole story?'

'I think I should.'

'Even if he considers you an interfering,
scaremongering, crazy young Englishwoman?'

'I don't care what he considers me, as long as he
is impressed enough to go and find out for himself.'

Piers nodded. 'That makes sense. But I don't
think you should go visiting the servants. It might
make things awkward for them if it were reported
or gossiped about by another servant. I have a
better idea. We'll send the *Dienstmann* with a
message that they should come and see you.'

'Who is the *Dienstmann*?'

'A man of many parts. There's one on the street-
corner here—you've seen him, wearing a kind of
képi and a jacket with epaulettes, and a metal
badge which gives his licence number.'

'What does he do?'

'Whatever you want. He will arrange anything.
You may have something to collect or deliver, or
want someone fetched to do a particular job—you
can trust him to do it. And he is very good and
discreet with messages. Shall I send him to ask the
old woman to come here?'

'That's a splendid idea.'

'Good! Now you can give your mind to the serious business of Christmas decorations.'

I made sure he fetched and carried for me, and we were making quite a good job of it, when he came back from getting some more greenery to find me on top of a step-ladder trying to fix the end of a garland over a large picture.

'Come down at once!' he ordered. 'The sight of a woman on a step-ladder terrifies me.'

'Don't worry. I am quite safe. I am just fixing this end.'

'No one should mount a step-ladder in an ankle-length skirt. It is highly dangerous!'

'I won't be a moment.'

'You certainly will not!'

Before I knew what was happening, he had seized me by the waist and lifted me down. Of course my skirt and foot became entangled in the foot of the step-ladder as he did so, and I nearly fell over. He held me, his arms tight and strong, while I regained my balance, and then, quite deliberately, he put his arms round me, bent his head and kissed me on the mouth. And it was no mere brushing of the lips; his mouth was firm and warm on mine, and it stayed there for several seconds while my heart suddenly bumped madly and my pulses throbbed. Strange, delightful sensations were running through me—my head began to spin—I rested in limp wonderment against his broad chest. Then, as his lips left mine, I remembered that his behaviour —and my inexplicable enjoyment of it—was both unconventional and totally reprehensible.

I began to push him away. My lips were tingling

and soft, and my heart thumping so hard that I could hardly speak.

'Piers! Let me go! What are you thinking of!'

Slowly he did so, looking quite unabashed, and answered coolly, 'There is mistletoe up there, is there not? A little Christmas custom . . .'

He spoke so confidently that I caught myself glancing upwards, although I knew there was just a garland—which was even more irritating! I retorted furiously, 'You know perfectly well there is none!'

'No? I could have sworn . . . In that case, accept my apologies—and remember this is a season of goodwill,' he added hastily, as I flashed him a look of outrage.

I decided it would be undignified to make a fuss. Perhaps it would take him down a peg by appearing totally unmoved by his action. I hoped he had not noticed that for a moment I went quite limp in his arms. He was giving me a long steady look.

'And what are you thinking about now?' I challenged him. 'Nothing on the previous lines, I hope?'

'Not quite. But I was thinking that the next opportunity to hold you in my arms will be at the Embassy Ball. May I book the supper dance now?'

'No, you may not! Oh, Mitzi was right!'

'Mitzi usually is. What did she say?'

'She said that you were sometimes quite outrageous, but pretended it was part of your soldierly ways, so that instead of being shocked, people just laughed.'

'Quite a good system, don't you think?'

It was impossible to put him out of face. I had to

find another reason for reproving him. 'Look! I was just fixing that garland, and now it has fallen down!'

'Then I shall see to it.'

He mounted the steps and did so, with his usual annoying efficiency, while I stood and wondered why my heart was still giving little excited thumps, my legs were feeling rather weak, and my cheeks, when I caught sight of myself in a mirror, were pinker than normal. After that, it was strange how often as we put up the rest of the decorations Piers's hand brushed mine—and each time my heart gave a little leap. I decided I must be turning into a weak and silly woman.

When we had finished, he turned to me and said, 'Well, Charlotte, have I earned the supper dance?'

I considered. 'Since I am acquainted with so few people here, perhaps I might as well settle for the devil I know. Very well.'

'The devil you know, eh? That's not very gracious!' He grinned. 'One of these days, if it's a devil you want, a devil you shall have.'

'And what does that mean?'

'Wait and see.'

'Oh, you are being provoking again!'

I might have pressed him, but at that moment a servant came in to tell me that a 'person' was asking to see me.

'What kind of person?'

'An elderly, humble type of woman, *Fräulein*.'

'That must be Adele's servant,' I said to Piers, then, to the servant, 'show her in, please.'

'In here, *Fräulein*?'

'Yes. I have asked her to come and see me.'

Old Marthe came in, rather diffidently, and looked warily at Piers.

'It's all right, Marthe,' I said. 'Captain Talbot is helping me, and knows about Baroness Adèle. I thought you would like to know that I have seen her. She is in hospital in Baden.'

'Ah, *gnädiges Fräulein*, how kind of you! And I have had good news—my young mistress is coming home for Christmas! The maids have been told to prepare for her and Baroness Elsa.'

'I am so pleased! She must be much better.'

So it was all a scare about nothing. Nevertheless . . .

'There is one thing I want to ask you. Do you know the name of Baroness Adèle's lawyer?'

'Her lawyer? Well, *Fräulein*, I ought to know. But he hasn't been to the Palace for years—not since the Baron died. I suppose, when they need to, they go to him. I can't remember—is it important?'

'I think it could be.'

'Well, I'll try to remember. And I'll ask Gottlieb —he may know. If I find out, I'll send to let you know. That's if we're here . . .' Her voice trailed off sadly.

'If you're here?'

'Baroness Elsa came yesterday, with the good news about my mistress, and bad news for us.'

She fumbled for a handkerchief and wiped her eyes.

'Oh, we're old, Gottlieb and I,' she went on, 'but we can still do our jobs. And—we've no children, so I live for my young mistress. It's going to be hard . . .' She choked on a sob.

'Why, what has happened?'

'We've been dismissed, that's what's happened! Well, not really dismissed, but pensioned off—but it feels the same to us. And you can call it a pension, but we can't live on it. We'll have to find some work, and what is there for an old couple like us, when there are younger folk who can't get jobs? I told the Baroness we can still work, to let us go on with our jobs while we're capable, but no, she said we must make way for younger people. We're being pushed out into the gutter, that's what it is, and what's more, by New Year. We have to find somewhere to live, and something to live on. But forgive me, *Fräulein*! I should not bother you with my troubles.'

'I'm glad you have told me. Piers, what can we do?'

'You have nowhere to go?' Piers asked her.

'No, sir. I'm trying to find a room, but . . .'

'You must let us know if you haven't found anything by the time you have to leave,' he said to her.

'In the meantime,' I added, 'we shall see what we can do. Does Baroness Adèle know about this?'

'I don't suppose so, *Fräulein*; she would never have allowed it. But now she can do nothing, whether she knows or not. I'm not allowed to serve her any more—she doesn't see either of us, ever. Well, we're the last of the old servants to go. She has no one but strangers around her now.'

'If you find somewhere to live, let us know where you will be. And let us know as soon as you find out the lawyer's name.'

'Yes, *gnädiges Fräulein*. A thousand thanks.'

She wiped her eyes again, bobbed us both a curtsy, and left.

I turned to Piers. 'What a heartless thing, to dismiss them like that, without enough pension to live on! And Marthe said something I didn't like. Did you notice it? She said they were the last of the old servants, that now Adèle will be cared for by strangers.'

'Yes,' Piers replied. 'But there need be nothing sinister in that. Old servants have eventually to be replaced, and all she means is that they are the last servants of Adèle's mother and the old Baron. To that old soul, anyone engaged later could be called a stranger.'

'I suppose so. But I didn't like it.'

'Don't see bogies where none exist, Charlotte! Adèle is coming home for Christmas, so that must be a good sign.'

'Yes. I am so relieved. Whatever happened at the hospital, she must have recovered from it. I shall send her a Christmas present. And I shall get something for New Year for Marthe. They will have Christmas at the Palace, but wouldn't it be a good idea to give them a New Year hamper to tide them over when they move?'

'That's a sound, practical thought.'

'Then I shall order it today. Do you think I could call on Adèle?'

'Charlotte, you're rushing fences again! Wait, she isn't home yet. You may have a chance to see her during Christmas.'

'There's no harm in my sending a present that Adèle can have when she arrives.'

'No harm at all. And now I must go. I shall

see you at the Ball. Are you going to shed your mourning?'

'Wait and see!'

'I don't need to. The look in your eyes tells me! *Auf wiedersehen*!'

I was trusting Piers now. Whether I had good reason, or whether it was just because I wanted to, I didn't know. And if it was foolish of me, I didn't care. He must be right, I told myself. I had been making a fuss over nothing. Adèle was coming home, she was better, she was not being coerced; she had simply exaggerated a natural desire to see her married into some kind of unwelcome pressure; now she would eat and get better and be a free agent. I was so determined to enjoy Christmas and not to worry myself or anyone else with my suspicions that I buried them all in the back of my brain. I even told myself that I had imagined the wine was drugged because I was too proud to admit I might have been drunk.

I deliberately forgot all disquieting thoughts, and went out shopping. With the coachman to take me to the best shops, and Tilde to escort me and ferry the parcels back to the carriage, I had a very succesful time. I bought a silk stole for Lady Bellanger, a cigar-box for Sir Thomas, and after much thought I settled on a shawl of fine lace for Adèle, which she could wear in bed, but which was lovely enough for any time she chose. I ordered the hamper for Marthe and Gottlieb, and I did not forget Tilde.

That left only Piers. I really ought to get him something, for he had been so patient and kind with me recently, in a matter which had nothing to do

with his normal duties. Another cigar-box? No.
Then what? It would not be correct to give him
anything personal, and yet I wanted to show a little
imagination. I was pleased when in a shop in Kärtnerstrasse I found something I thought would
appeal to him—a carved wooden figure of a
cavalryman with his horse. He was dismounted,
and had one hand on the horse's muzzle in an
attitude so natural that you believed he was talking
to the animal as he caressed it.

As we returned to the carriage, Tilde asked,
'Aren't you going to see the crib at Stephansdom,
Fräulein?'

I guessed that she wanted to see it.

'What a good idea, Tilde!'

So the coachman turned the carriage, and we
threaded our way along Kärtnerstrasse, its gutters
lined with piles of snow, the pavements full of
people wrapped up against the cold, hurrying and
bustling by, while the shop windows glowed with
lovely things, and above us golden lights brightened the winter dusk. And there was St Stephen's,
lifting its curious herringbone-patterned roof
above the newer buildings. The great church was
decked in Christmas finery, starred with points of
light from hundreds of candles; everywhere it
seemed to glow with the message of love. The
Christmas Crib was touching in its simplicity and
beauty, and I was glad Tilde had reminded me
about it. I felt a glow of happiness spreading
through me—everything was going to turn out
well. It was going to be a happy Christmas. I could
not mourn my father for ever; he had died doing
what he believed was his duty to a girl he had never

seen before, and I must accept it.

My present to Adèle was beautifully wrapped, and I sent it round to the Palace with a brief note. I had the final fitting for my ball-gown; I wrote cards to go with my other presents. I took a ridiculously long time wondering what to put on Piers's card. My feelings for him had changed, and I had to admit he was no longer stiff and unapproachable, and my feuds with him seemed rather silly.

In the end I wrote:

> A peace-offering. Goodwill from Charlotte.

I hoped he would understand.

And everything was turning out right. Two days before the Ball, I had a note on crested paper from the Phoenix Palace. It was from Adèle, and read:

> Thank you for your beautiful present. I hope I shall see you soon.
> Adèle.

I could not wait. Adèle's note, I decided, was as good as an invitation. The next afternoon, at what I hoped was At Home time, I called at the Palace. Gottlieb opened the door to me, and told a lounging footman to take my name and see if I could be received. While he was upstairs, I made the opportunity to exchange a few words with Gottlieb.

'So the Baroness Adèle is back! That's good, isn't it?'

'I'm not too sure, *Fräulein*. Of course, we haven't seen her, me and Marthe. We're not allowed a glimpse, mustn't go near her. It's a queer business, this taking her to and fro, when if they left her in peace she'd fancy her food again and soon be well.'

'Gottlieb, what do you know of Count Palkany? Is he often here?'

That wary, almost frightened look with which I was getting too familiar came into his eyes.

'He's—he's a friend of the young master. Lieutenant Szarvas sees a lot of him, so he's here pretty often.'

'He has an estate near Marienwald, hasn't he?'

'Has he? Well, they've all got their country lodges, these young bloods.'

'Did you see my father some months ago? He must have come here.'

He scratched his head thoughtfully, and said nothing. I was sure he was considering what was prudent, or safe, to tell me.

'Please, Gottlieb, there's no harm in telling me?'

'Well, *Fräulein*,' he said grudgingly. 'He came, just the once. The Baroness Elsa was out, so Marthe managed to get him to see the Baroness Adèle—but very soon *she* came back, and went up, and found him with her. Soon after he came down. On his way out, he spoke to me.'

'What did he say?'

'He just said, "Look after her, Gottlieb. I'll do what I can."'

'That was all?'

'That was all, and I never saw him again.'

'But you heard about his death?'

'We weren't sure. We only saw a line or two in the paper, that a foreigner had died, accidentally, in a hunting party. It didn't give a name or say just where it had happened. A bit queer, we thought, to say so little—but the papers are full of deaths. We had no real reason to think it was the milord. Only he never came back, and from that time they guarded my mistress like a prisoner.'

The footman reappeared at the top of the great flight of steps, and Gottlieb muttered a few more words to me.

'That Palkany, *Fräulein*—take care. He's worse than Lieutenant Szarvas!'

We waited in silence for the footman to reach us. He bowed to me and said, 'The Baroness will receive milady.'

My spirits rose at once. I was going to see Adèle!

I followed the footman upstairs and through the salons feeling happier than I had done for weeks. I was shown into the little salon, and my name was announced. I found myself face to face, not with Adèle, but with her stepmother.

Lieutenant Szarvas was also in the room. I greeted them both, and he placed a chair for me. We exchanged the usual civilities, and then I asked after Adèle.

'Oh, she is better after her relapse,' said Baroness Elsa lightly, as though Adèle's health was quite a trivial matter. 'She is resting in her room. The servants have instructions not to disturb her if she is sleeping. If she wakes in time, she will come and join us for tea.'

So my delight was shortlived: at this my spirits plummeted, and for no reason I felt not only disappointment but disgust.

'Did you enjoy your stay in Baden?' asked the Baroness sweetly.

I tried to be self-possessed—of course she must

know I had visited Adèle. 'Very much. But I expect Vienna will be more exciting during Christmas.'

'Vienna is always more exciting,' Szarvas drawled. 'Well, Christmas is nearly here, and soon after that it will be *Fasching*—and during *Fasching* anything can happen. When it's a good *Fasching*, the whole city goes mad.'

The door opened, and the footman announced Countess Plesch and Count Palkany. She swept in, trailing a cloak of mulberry silk, followed by Palkany with a jingle of spurs, a gleam of gold lace and the flash of bright metal. He unhooked his wolf-skin and tossed it on a chair, greeted the Baroness and myself, and then took a chair beside me. Meanwhile the Countess Plesch had subsided on to the sofa beside the Baroness, exclaiming that she was totally exhausted by Christmas shopping.

'One needs the strength of an ox! Darling Elsa, a cup of your tea is exactly what I need. And Sachertorte—what could be better?'

She helped herself to the rich chocolate cake.

'Shall you be here for Carnival, Lady Charlotte?' Baroness Elsa asked.

'I hope so,' I replied. 'I should like to stay, for we have nothing similar in England.'

'Then you *must* see it,' the Countess insisted.

'Yes, you will find Vienna full of surprises at *Fasching*,' said Palkany.

Tea being too innocuous for him, he had accepted a glass of brandy, which he now began to drink, eyeing me boldly over the rim of the glass as he did so.

'Are you going to the British Embassy Ball, Lady Charlotte?' Szarvas asked.

'I expect so.'

I could see why Mitzi had said that the Baroness was besotted with Palkany: she could not take her eyes off him, she hung on every word, and her cheeks had heightened colour. It was a little ridiculous, I thought, for she was some years older than he, and twice a widow—though I supposed that would make no difference to a woman if she was in love. She must have been very young when first married, and was, as Adèle had said, considerably younger than her second husband, Adèle's father. She was still a pretty woman, with her blonde hair and blue eyes and attractive rounded figure—it was uncharitable of me to think she looked like a somewhat ageing china doll.

And that, I thought, was how Palkany would treat her, as a doll to be played with, a puppet to dance as he pulled the strings, a toy to be thrown aside as soon as she was no more use to him. I could see no trace of kindness or consideration in that face as he sat there smiling and drinking; he looked more wolfish than ever. Szarvas, too, although he looked like a boy overtaken by early dissipation, lacked any of the softness of youth. He might not be as ruthless, but he could be equally cruel. With sudden intuition, I thought the difference between the two men was that Palkany was vicious and strong, while Szarvas was vicious and weak.

Palkany turned to me again. 'It seems our paths were destined to cross ever since we first saw you on the Orient Express,' he said smoothly. 'Who knows what reason Fate may have for that?'

'Do you believe in Fate, Count Palkany?' I retorted, as coolly as I could. 'Personally, I think we make our own fate by our actions.'

'Oh, indeed, I agree with you up to a point. But sometimes an attempt to influence the course of events can recoil on one's own head. It is always dangerous to meddle in a situation one does not fully understand.'

His lips smiled, but the cold glitter in his eyes made his words sound like a threat. A threat to me, not to meddle in Adele's affairs? Or was it perhaps a judgment passed on my father's actions? I felt a shiver of fear, and at the same time a surge of cold anger.

'It does not seem as if Adèle is taking tea,' said Baroness Elsa.

No, I thought, because you have forbidden it.

'Oh, what a pity,' Countess Plesch remarked. 'I should have liked to see her now that she is improving. So sad, that her illness should have dragged on like this.'

'I assure you, Mama does not intend to let things go on like this much longer,' Szarvas told her, almost petulantly.

I decided that as Adèle was not expected, I had better leave, and stood up to make my adieux.

'*Auf wiedersehen*, Lady Charlotte,' said Palkany. 'Who knows where we may meet again? At a ball—a Carnival occasion—even a wedding, perhaps?'

'Why, is someone at the British Embassy getting married?' the Countess interposed.

'I have no idea,' replied Palkany, his voice like silk. 'I always say marriage is like measles, you never know where it may break out.'

I did not like it. Perhaps it was my over-active

imagination, but everything Palkany said seemed to have a note of menace. I tried to analyse the look on each face as we said our goodbyes. Szarvas, curious; Palkany, contemptuous, almost insolent; the Countess, confident and challenging; Baroness Elsa, indifferent; she still had eyes only for Palkany.

The footman was waiting outside. As he closed the door behind me, I heard a burst of derisive laughter, which seemed to follow me as I walked away. I told myself it was only the sudden cold of the outer rooms that sent a shiver down my back and made me want to hurry out of the Palace and back to somewhere warm, familiar, reassuring.

I was driven home, but even in Lady Bellanger's pretty drawing-room I found that laughter still ringing in my ears.

CHAPTER SEVEN

THE NEXT morning I was almost sure that I had been letting my imagination get the better of me. Adèle's health was improving, and she was back in her home. Why should I let her absence from the drawing-room, and the arrival of Palkany and the Countess on a friendly call, seem sinister? Why should I read darker meanings into their superficial chatter? The way was still open for me to call on Adèle again, and I would certainly do so. Perhaps, next time, I would manage to see her.

It was the day of the Embassy Ball, and that event took all my attention. My life had been so quiet in the past months that I was caught in greater than normal anticipation. I did not hope that my dance-card would be filled, but I intended to enjoy myself nevertheless. And Piers had booked the supper dance, which meant I should have an escort at the important time. Sir Thomas would certainly ask me for one dance—he was punctilious, and an agreeable man—and I had met one or two of the Embassy staff when Piers took me skating who might also claim dances. The rest of the time I would be content to watch.

As it happened, I had as many partners as I could cope with. I imagined it was because I was a new-comer, for in the relatively restricted society a new face would be welcome; for whatever reason, I was positively besieged with requests to fill the spaces on my card. I kept one dance late in the second half of the programme free for emergencies.

The Embassy was quite splendid, it made me wish I had had a proper season when I 'came out', for there was something very enjoyable in dressing up in one's best finery and going off to dance to lovely music in opulent surroundings. I had not had enough of such occasions to be accustomed to them.

'I quite forgot to tell you, Charlotte,' said Lady Bellanger, 'about one quaint custom here. At a ball there is always a room called the *Comtessen-Zimmer*, which is set aside for the unmarried girls. They go there between dances and chatter away, and no married lady will dare to set foot inside! Even here in the Embassy the custom is observed. You may use it or not, as you wish.'

I thought it might be amusing to do so.

Never before had I seen such an array of uniforms! They far outnumbered formal evening dress on the men, and there was such an incredible variety that it seemed as though every European nation must be represented. Many of the ladies, by contrast, were still in mourning or half-mourning, but the richness of their toilettes was not in any way diminished: they were swirling with ostrich feathers in black, purple, silver grey or violet, sparkling with black sequins and jet beads, gleaming with grey pearls. In fact I thought that against a scarlet English tunic or a sky-blue Hussar uniform, the mourning toilettes were very effective.

I watched as around me the colours shifted and swirled, overhead the great chandeliers glowed and glittered, and the movement on the polished floor set up a constant rustle of silk and satin. As we had walked towards the ballroom I had begun to hear music, at first only faint snatches under the buzz of conversation, then growing louder, more continuous, more distinguishable, till at the entrance to the ballroom it burst upon me in a wonderful tide of melody, swinging along with a lilt and a sparkle such as I had never heard before. It was irresistible —all one wanted to do was to dance. I caught my breath—so *this* was Viennese music! It made all the Victorian waltzes of English composers seem like insignificant pallid trivialities; this was the essence of life transformed into dance time. I had heard Strauss waltzes played in London, but never like this!

'Good evening, Charlotte. You look as if you want a partner.'

It was Piers, smiling down at me with open admiration.

'And out of mourning, I see,' he went on, before I had the chance to reply. 'May I say it becomes you?'

'Good evening, Piers. You may, for I always enjoy a compliment. And, yes, I should love a partner.'

'Well, here is one for you, waiting to be introduced—but you must not love him, for he is an unregenerate rascal. But he is a good dancer. So may I present Henry Dalrymple?'

He did not look much of a rascal—just a good-looking, fair, fresh-faced Englishman. It was a change to meet someone who did not have a title. In Viennese society, everyone I met seemed to be a count or a baroness—and I said so.

'Well, I have only a little one,' he admitted with an engaging smile.

'He is a mere Honourable. You illogical creature —you have a title yourself!'

'But I am used to that! Well, I shall discount the Honourable, and give you a dance.'

'Don't forget, Charlotte, the supper dance is mine,' Piers put in.

The time sped by on dancing feet. Polkas, mazurkas, waltzes—I danced them all. Oh, the waltzes! They were sheer bliss, and I found myself thinking, the supper dance is a waltz. I caught glimpses of Piers, always dancing with a different partner, tall and straight and broad-shouldered, his dress uniform fitting like a glove, and I wondered how I could ever have thought him bad-tempered, stuffy, and almost middle-aged. He was thirty, a splendid age for a man, and when he had been cross it had been my fault—I must have tried his temper sorely. I probably would again, but that had nothing to do with it. As for being stuffy—Mitzi was right. He was outrageous, he had told me I ought to be spanked, and that he was thinking of holding me in his arms at the Embassy Ball. In the meantime I was never short of a partner; some were more agreeable than others, but I enjoyed each dance. And in due course the supper dance came.

For a moment I thought, He's forgotten, he's talking to someone else—but then I saw his head topping the others round me and he came forward with hand outstretched.

'My dance.'

I smiled, and our hands met. There was a long and lovely introduction to the music as he led me on to the floor, and then in a great sweep of harmony the orchestra swung into waltz time. One hand held mine, the other clasped my waist, we were swaying and swinging and circling to the beat of the music. Scores of other couples swayed and swung, but I thought only of Piers as his head bent a little to mine, his lips smiled at me, his clear eyes gazed into my face.

'I do believe you are enjoying yourself, Charlotte,' he murmured.

'Dancing to a Strauss waltz, played like this, in Vienna—it's like being in heaven!' I replied.

'Not quite, I hope!' he retorted. 'You are not looking angelic. You are human, real—full of life and fascination—and you are in my arms. I've no wish to hold an angel, there's no future in that!'

The arm at my waist tightened a fraction as we swirled around, and strange sensations coursed through my body. I had no idea if he was talking sense or nonsense, but it was thrilling, and he had called me fascinating.

'Future?' I whispered.

'Angels disappear. You will stay, to dance with me again. You will, won't you?'

'Yes, Piers.'

'Good. After Christmas we have Carnival, and we shall dance till we drop. Then we'll drink champagne and dance again.'

I could think of nothing better. I was dizzy with the dancing, drunk with the music—and I was falling in love.

We said no more until the waltz ended in a breathtaking acceleration before the final chords, and Piers steadied me and then let me go. The next moment he offered me his arm.

'Supper, I think? And champagne—unless you prefer some other wine?'

'No, champagne! It is so light and delicious.'

'Charlotte, will you give me another dance tonight?'

I pretended to consider. 'Ought I? And I have only one left . . .'

'Splendid! I'll take it.'

'You arrogant man! Suppose I don't wish to?'

'In that case you wouldn't have told me. What is it—another waltz?'

'A mazurka.'

'Thank heaven it is not a polka! To polka with such a young and vigorous partner might well leave me in a state of collapse. A mazurka I can manage.'

'Oh, Piers, what nonsense!' I laughed. 'After that waltz, to talk like an old gentleman!'

He looked at me quizzically. 'Isn't that what I am to you?'

'Of course not! You're . . .' I caught myself up just in time. I was about to say, You're just the right age to me. I added lamely, 'You're a very good age, I should think—not too young, but not old.'

We might have said more, but at that moment we were confronted by Count Palkany, who greeted us both very pleasantly, and then addressed me.

'Lady Charlotte, will you do me the honour of granting me a dance?'

'I am so sorry, Count, but my card is full.'

'You are too late, Palkany!' Piers told him. 'Lady Charlotte is in great demand.'

'How singularly unfortunate I am. I shall hope for better luck during *Fasching*, when ladies evade their watchdogs and become more accessible.'

He moved away, and I suppressed a sigh of relief. Somehow I always felt apprehensive when he was near.

'So I'm a watchdog, am I?' said Piers. 'And a good thing too, for I think you don't care for him.'

'I do not. There's something about him—something menacing.'

'Menacing? Not to you, surely? But he's a slippery customer, and a danger to women—so don't give him more than one dance!'

'I hope not to give him any. To dance with him would feel like sharing a joint of meat with a wolf.'

A wolf—I always came back to that.

'Your vivid imagination again! Well, quieten such thoughts—here is food and drink, and the only wolves about are very tame ones! Young Dalrymple, for example.'

'You said he was an unregenerate rascal!'

'Only to please him. He thinks young ladies like a man with an aura of wickedness.'

'And do they?'

'You must tell me—I've never been able to decide. Would you like me more if I said I had gambled away a fortune and killed a man in an illicit duel?'

'Don't fish! I should probably like—or dislike —you just as I do now.'

After supper, dancing was resumed, and at one point I went to the *Comtessen-Zimmer* to pin up my hair and indulge my curiosity. It was full of young girls, all chattering and giggling and exchanging views on their partners. Some of the remarks I heard would have shocked the stately mamas sitting around the fringe of the ballroom. I had met some of the girls, and they accepted me, assuming that like them I was embarking on the hunt for a husband.

'I saw you had the supper dance with Captain Talbot!' said one of them. 'How beautifully he waltzes—quite like a Viennese! But are you serious about him? You may be wasting your time!'

'*Serious?* I hardly think so!'

'He has the reputation of being a confirmed bachelor. He can flirt very agreeably, but it's quite strange for a man of his age that although he's quite appreciative he's not been known to have a thorough *affaire*—and there are several married ladies who would be willing to fall into his arms, I'm told. Perhaps he's terribly deep and secret? For, though they say Englishmen are cold, I don't think *he* is.'

I wanted to ask her why, but she rattled off on to something else. Then—I don't know how— Adèle's name was mentioned.

'We never see her now,' said another girl.

'No. Last year she was at most of the balls—but that was before she fell ill.'

'*And* before it was proposed that she should marry Erich Szarvas! Do you think it was just a coincidence?'

'Would *you* mind marrying him?'

'Oh, I don't think so. He's a good-looking, and quite agreeable—much the same as most.'

'He hasn't much money.'

'But he has a very nice estate from his father, in Hungary, I'm told. And I dare say his mother would be generous.'

The girls were singularly undemanding in their husband-hunting, I thought.

'I heard a rumour that visitors were not allowed to see Adèle because she is rather *strange*,' said the first girl meaningfully.

'Are you saying she's not right in the head? How dreadful!'

'Not as bad as that, but—strange. Definitely a little odd.'

I could not let that pass. 'As a matter of fact,' I said, 'I saw Baroness Adèle quite recently, and she is perfectly normal. Her health is delicate, that is all.'

'Oh? Well, that's not so bad.'

I was not sure that I had convinced them. I was not even sure I had convinced myself, but once again I thrust aside my doubts. When I returned to the dancing, the music dispelled any troubling thoughts, it was all happiness, frivolity, enjoyment. In the last mazurka—a dance which shows up a partner's bearing and needs both manliness and elegance—Piers looked the perfection of soldierliness and grace.

When it was all over and the carriage had borne us home, I fell into bed feeling like one of the dancing princesses in the fairy-tale, and slept soundly until nearly noon.

It seemed strange to be spending Christmas in Vienna, yet I did not miss England. Had I been there, I should have felt most acutely the loss of my father; I should have been obliged to go to the aunts, and they would have made even more of it. Here I could join in the celebrations in a different setting, and the Bellangers were a kindly couple, determined to make me as happy as possible. We exchanged presents as if we were a family, round a Christmas tree; and to my surprise, there was an extra parcel bearing my name.

Inside was a beautiful pair of long pale grey kid gloves with tiny silver buttons, and tucked between them, another little packet. This was most thoroughly wrapped, and when I opened it I found it was a gingerbread man! Attached to him was a little card which read:

> Sugar and spice and all things nice—that's what Charlotte is made of. Piers.

And the gloves fitted. He was a most surprising man.

So with parties and balls the days sped by. All at once it was New Year's Eve—and a little warmer, with a damp clinging fog in the streets that made one want to see the New Year in indoors before a well-stoked stove. New Year's Eve, and I had heard nothing from Adèle, and nothing from her servants. Up to now I had considered that no news was good news; perhaps it was the depressing fog which made me melancholy, for I began to ask myself, what was I doing here?

I had discovered that Adèle had asked for help to save her from an unwelcome marriage; I had found out that my father died in a hunting accident; now Adèle seemed to be improving and not under coercion, so what more did I hope to do? Surely I could discount her nervousness? She was, after all, very frail. I had very little excuse for staying on in Vienna—except for a silly uneasiness for a girl who had no claim on me, and now, a feeling of affection for a man who was a confirmed bachelor and looked on me as a wilful girl. He had sent me a pair of gloves and a sweet message, but I must not make too much of that. At Christmas time such a gift could be made without significance. He was a flirt, so I had been told; it seemed he did not want any kind of serious relationship with a woman.

I supposed I should be glad that he had not had one of those *affaires* which the Viennese took so lightly. Glad? It was nothing to do with me—I was not going to fall in love with him! That would be disastrous, for sooner or later I must go back to England and forget him. It would be far more sensible to avoid seeing him more than necessary, for I was finding those clear grey eyes, so light against his black lashes and dark skin, that quizzical smile, the air of strength in that tall lean frame becoming more and more disturbing to my peace of mind. Still, I had no need to be precipitate. I had been invited to stay and see *Fasching*, and in less than a week, on the sixth of January, Carnival would begin. But before *Fasching* opened, the fragile peace I had built up for myself was abruptly shattered.

A note came for me—another of those cheap, slightly grubby envelopes. I opened it with a feeling of foreboding. Again the message was short:

> They took her away last night. We heard her crying out as she went. Today we were turned out of doors. We have been given shelter here. We thank you from the bottom of our hearts for the food.

There was an address at the top which meant

nothing to me. I reread the note, and shivered. I
decided at once that I must speak to Marthe or
Gottlieb in person.

First, I would have to find them. Wherever their
room was, it would not be in a fashionable quarter,
so although I could hire a cab, it was probably not
the sort of district where an upper-class girl should
go by herself. I was prepared to go. While an
upper-class Viennese girl was not allowed to go
anywhere by herself, I was English, and therefore,
I thought, entitled to some eccentricity. But, all the
same, there were limits. The poor quarters could be
unsafe, one risked having one's purse or jewellery
snatched even inside a building.

So I would have to ask Piers to go with me.
Mentally I rebelled at this. I felt he might obstruct
me—for my own good, he would say—and, besides, this was a private matter which I would prefer
to pursue alone. And why should a woman always
be dependent on a man? It seemed that men had
arranged things so that women could do nothing
without them. Adèle's money was a case in point.
Adèle—Adèle, taken from the Palace, crying out
—taken God knows where. To Baden again? One
could not be sure. 'Next time, it would be somewhere worse . . .' Wherever she was, I must find
her. *How?* Piers. When information was needed,
or protection wanted in a rough quarter, it had to
be Piers.

He called that afternoon; had he not done so, I
should have sent a message to the Embassy. I
showed him Marthe's letter, and he read it, frown-
ing. 'It doesn't say where she has been taken.'

'*They don't know!* Oh, Piers, I am sure there is

something very wrong. I want to go and see them to find out all they can tell me. Will you take me?'

'Yes. But, Charlotte, if we find out anything, you must not rush off and do something precipitate.'

'Very well, Piers.' I could look and sound submissive when necessary.

Piers must have made a good excuse, since Lady Bellanger did not seem to mind him escorting me, and we set off in a cab together. Although I had expected the address to be in a poor quarter, even so I was amazed at what I saw. It was quite a long drive from the heart of Vienna to the suburb, and here poverty was all too evident. It was a rabbit-warren of old houses, ill kept, out of repair, the narrow streets full of rubbish and crowded with people dressed in all sorts of shabby, threadbare, patched, ragged garments—and generally not enough of them in this damp, bitter, weather. As they walked, they crouched in a vain attempt to keep warm, their hands in their flimsy coats or under their armpits, their faces red or blue with cold, their features pinched with hunger and despair. I could hardly bear to look out of the cab window.

'Piers, this is dreadful!' I whispered.

'Yes. It is the other side I told you about. But I assure you it is not peculiar to Vienna. I don't suppose you have ever been into the poor districts of London?'

I shook my head.

The cab stopped by a group of tall old buildings. Unpainted and ramshackle, the house was no worse and no better than any of the others. Piers asked a question of a woman who had just thrown some slops out of the door. She shook her head, and was going inside when she turned back, said a few words, and pointed upstairs. Piers turned back to me.

'She didn't know the name, but then remembered that someone on the fourth has just been joined by an old couple.'

He told the cabbie to wait, and we went up —somewhat gingerly on my part, for the stone steps were slippery with damp and the occasional patch of trodden-in refuse, and the banister greasy and unsafe. Piers kept his hand on my arm, while I held my skirts clear of the unwholesome stair. There was an unpleasant smell everywhere: rancid, rotten, the stench of years of poverty and decay.

When we reached the fourth floor, Piers knocked at the first door. It opened, and a thin, untidy, unshaven man shook his head at Piers's question. Then a little urchin appeared and piped up the information that in the third room there were two strangers. We went there; knocked; and the door was opened by a woman with a small child in her arms. She looked too weary even to be surprised at the sight of us, but when Piers asked for Marthe and Gottlieb she nodded and called back into the room. Marthe appeared.

'Oh, milady! Milord! I never thought you'd come here!'

'I must talk to you, Marthe,' I began.

'Come inside.'

She showed us into a room, cleaner than might be expected, and set two old wooden chairs for us—the only chairs I could see. I tried not to look about me, but was aware that beside a table and a shelf or two on the wall there was little in the room but a couple of bundles of old blankets.

The woman with the child looked at Marthe. 'I expect it's private,' she said. 'I'll go across to Frau Hummell.'

It showed a delicacy I had not expected.

'That's my niece,' said Marthe. 'She's a good girl. She took us in, bless her—I don't know what we'd have done otherwise. But, *gnädiges Fräulein*, I had to write to you! It's my little mistress—I'm nearly out of my mind thinking of her . . .'

'Tell us exactly what happened,' I said.

'There's so little to tell! It was late in the evening when a closed carriage arrived and was driven inside. Two women—hard-faced creatures, big and strapping they were—got out, and the new footman took them upstairs. A bit later they came down, carrying my little mistress! She was all wrapped up in blankets, so tight she couldn't move, but she was throwing her head from side to side and crying out. "No! No!" she was calling. "You mustn't take me—you can't take me!" But they paid no heed to her, and there was the Baroness Elsa behind them saying, "It's all arranged, Adèle, it's for your own good. You can come home as soon as you are better and have got rid of those silly ideas."'

Marthe stopped to wipe her eyes, and choked on a sob.

'I was hiding in the shadow of the door,' she went on, 'and I could see her—the Baroness Elsa—she was *smiling*! "You've no reason to make a fuss," she said. "You'll be well looked after."' They bundled Baroness Adèle into the carriage and got in, the two women, and drove away. The Baroness Elsa went upstairs like a cat who'd been at the cream. And that was that.'

My heart was thumping and my hands were clammy.

'And couldn't you find out anything?' I asked.

'Oh, milady, as soon as I could, I asked the footman where they had taken her, and he said it was none of my business! No one would tell us anything. And then—then we were turned out, with what she called our first pension money. To me it was like thirty pieces of silver!'

She burst into tears, burying her face in her apron. I stood up and put my arm round her.

'Marthe, you mustn't be so upset. You haven't betrayed Adèle—quite the reverse. You have done all you could, you have told me, and now I must think what is best to be done.'

Actually I could think of nothing, but I patted her shoulder while she scrubbed her face, and her reddened eyes in their network of wrinkles looked at me pleadingly.

'You will help, milady? You'll find her? You'll get her away from those people?'

'I will if I possibly can. I'll do my best. I'm very concerned about her, Marthe.'

'Yes, yes.'

She sniffed and wiped her face again.

'Of course you're concerned! So you would be, for your own flesh and blood.'

CHAPTER EIGHT

POOR OLD thing! I thought. She's upset, her mind is muddled, her memory playing her false.

'Flesh and blood, Marthe? No, we're not related. But I care very much for Adèle,' I said gently.

She stared at me open-mouthed. 'Milady! You don't know? Oh, what have I said!'

Piers did not utter a word, but got to his feet and I felt his hand under my arm, supporting me. I vaguely wondered why. My mind was suddenly busy with what Marthe had said.

'Marthe—what do you mean? You had better tell me.'

Doubt and worry showed in her face as she looked from me to Piers.

'If you know something, Marthe; if you are quite sure, I think you should tell Lady Charlotte,' he said quietly.

'Oh, milady, I didn't think you would have come unless you knew. I thought milord Hilary must have told you . . .'

'Told me what, Marthe?'

My stomach was sinking; my body suddenly felt hollow; I was glad of Piers's arm. I was afraid, and did not know what I feared.

'That you and my little mistress . . . You are half-sisters.'

At first I simply could not take it in. My father —myself—Adèle—*no!* I could not believe it, I would not believe it. My horror and incredulity must have been obvious, for Piers sat me down on the rickety chair and began to talk to me, gently, sensibly.

'Don't think about it now, Charlotte. For the time being, let it pass. Remember that we are here to help Adèle. She needs help, and it seems we are the only people ready and capable of doing anything. Just think of that.'

I nodded dumbly, not knowing what to do next. I had lost my powers of reasoning.

Mercifully Piers had not. He turned to Marthe. 'You must try to find out the name of Baroness Adèle's lawyer. It is most important now.'

'I'll try . . . I'll try, milord.'

'Thank you, Marthe. Do you need any help yourself at present?'

'No, milord, we can manage.'

'Keep in touch with us. Now, if there is nothing more you can tell us about the Baroness, I think we had better leave.'

'Not for a moment! I must tell the *gnädiges Fräulein* about it—she looks so upset! Oh, milday, they loved each other so much, your papa and the Baroness Steffi! They would have married, but it was not possible—her family had promised her to Baron Feldbach. I helped them to meet a few times—I was her maid, you know—and there was nothing more than a kiss between them. But at the last, before he went away . . . Oh, milady, it was how they both wanted it!'

I put my hands over my ears, but she took no notice and I could still hear her talking.

'She was so happy, and no one but me knew that

little Adèle was *his* daughter. It was the only way she could keep the baby. Before she died, she made me promise to look after little Adèle, and if she needed help and there was no other way, she was to write to milord. Oh, *Fräulein*, she has no one now—no one but you . . .'

I nodded in dumb misery, and let Piers lead me away, out of that wretched room, down that greasy foetid stair, and into the cab. He settled me in the corner and tucked a rug round me. Neither of us spoke for a long time.

When I had pulled myself together to some extent, I said, 'Piers, what can we do? How can we find Adèle?'

'I've been thinking about that. I shall telegraph Mitzi and ask her to make enquiries at the hospitals in Baden to see if she has been taken there again. I can check in the Vienna hospitals, and I will try to find out, by very discreet enquiries, the name of Adèle's lawyer. That, I think, is all we can do for a start.'

I felt slightly relieved. Piers was not being obstructive now, but was really helping.

'Thank you, Piers. Suddenly I feel so—useless.'

'Well, it's a difficult situation. And you've had a shock. Try to get a good night's sleep, and every-thing will look better in the morning.'

But it didn't. I slept badly, and in the morning I woke with a raging headache, a sore throat and the feeling that I had been put through a mangle several times, very roughly. Tilde took one look at me and called Lady Bellanger; she took one look at me and summoned the doctor.

For three days the doctor came twice a day. I lay

in a state of utter wretchedness, unable to eat,
wanting to drink to ease my painful throat, though
every swallow was an agony. If I slept, I was
haunted by nightmares. The third day, the doctor
said to Lady Bellanger, 'We can be thankful it is not
diphtheria.'

At least I shan't choke to death, I thought—but
felt survival was still uncertain. I am not a sickly
person, and I could not remember ever feeling so
ill. What it was I do not know—perhaps as a visitor
I was susceptible to some infection that did not
seriously trouble the residents. I only know that
I lay there, feverish and aching, my head full
of muddled thoughts to which I could give no
coherence, my general torment increased by the
noises from the street. I had not realised Vienna
could be so noisy. Always there seemed to be
people shouting and laughing, drums banging,
whistles screaming, rattles crackling in an unending
cacophony. Or was I imagining it? Was it all part of
the strange waking nightmare I seemed to be in? I
was too ill even to ask.

Lady Bellanger told me that Piers called every
day to enquire how I was, and there were always
flowers from him in my room, though it was about
ten days before I was able to appreciate these
attentions. Then I gradually improved: my
headache and sore throat subsided, and one morning I felt considerably better. Tilde helped me to
wash, and then between us we tried to arrange my
hair. I looked at myself in the hand-mirror and was
shocked.

At my expression, she said, 'Don't worry,
milady. Of course you do not look well yet—you

have hardly eaten for two weeks! But with good light food you will soon pick up, and your cheeks will fill out and get their colour back again.'

It was not the fact that I still looked ill that had startled me. The face I saw in the mirror was not Charlotte Brantham's—it was Adèle's. My own face, now so much thinner, with hollows in the cheeks and an unnaturally pale skin bore an uncanny resemblance to hers. We could be sisters.

We *were* sisters! I could not doubt Marthe's story. And I felt afresh the shock, the dreadful stab of pain, the agonising thoughts her words had brought me. I wanted nothing more to do with Adèle. I thought I hated her. But I was now well enough to wonder what had happened to her.

It was mid-afternoon on that day when Lady Bellanger came in to ask if I felt well enough to have a visitor.

'It is unconventional, my dear, but Piers is so anxious to see you. He has been very worried about you.'

When and why did she start calling him Piers and giving him privileges? I wondered in passing. I told her I should like to see him. He came in looking very grave, but a smile of relief appeared when he saw me sitting in bed propped up with pillows and not at death's door.

'Charlotte, what a fright you've given me!'

He took my hand and sat down by the bed. He seemed to be in no hurry to let go, and I found the warm pressure of his fingers very comforting.

'Are you really better?' he asked.

'Much better. I am going to be allowed to sit up in a chair for a little while tomorrow.'

'I'm very glad. The truth is, I've missed you, and all the alarms and excursions you've given me! Life has been dull.'

'Thank you for all the flowers, Piers. It was so kind of you.'

'Kind! A few flowers!'

His eyes gazed into mine. I supposed it was just weakness that gave me a strange fluttering feeling inside. I decided it was time I took my hand back, and did so. He clasped his strong lean brown ones together on the edge of the bed and still looked at me.

'Lady Bellanger says I must not stay long, so I had better tell you what I have found out—or rather, what I have *not* found out,' he went on.

I looked at him enquiringly.

'Mitzi says she is unable to trace Adèle in any of the Baden hospitals. Similarly, I have been unable to find her in any in Vienna. She must have been taken away to a small private nursing-home, or even a private house. I am at a loss to know what to do. Our best bet is to identify her lawyer, but my discreet enquiries are taking a long time, and no one has found out his name yet.'

Adèle—Adèle—I turned my head away from him and shut my eyes, but even so two little tears squeezed out and began to trickle down my cheeks.

'Oh, Charlotte, don't cry! We'll think of something—we'll find her.'

I turned back to him. 'It isn't that. Of course we must find her, but it's the other thing that is upsetting me . . .'

'The other thing?'

It was impossible to keep my anguish inside

myself any longer. 'My father—that's what hurts. How *could* he!'

Piers took possession of my hand again.

'I see. Now, Charlotte, it's natural that you should be upset. But you're grown up, and you must stop believing in fairy-tales. In real life, love is different. It's not always happy ever after.' His voice was gentle in spite of its firmness.

'I know that. But the facts—you can't explain them away! He loved that other woman—she was having his child, and he left her—then he married my mother and pretended he loved *her* for the rest of his life!'

'Pretended? Charlotte, be honest. You believed he loved your mother, didn't you—until now?'

'Yes.'

'And do you think, in all those years you lived with him, you wouldn't have suspected if it had been otherwise? Children sense things very accurately.'

'Then, if he loved my mother, how can you explain the rest?'

'I can. I have had another talk with Marthe, which made things very clear. You must listen to me calmly and do your best to understand. Will you?'

I nodded.

'Try to go back in time and think of your father as a young man, a very young man. He comes to Vienna, he meets a charming girl and falls head over heels in love. That's perfectly natural. Then he discovers that a marriage has already been arranged for her. He finds out that she does not love this man. He thinks she should break the

engagement and marry him, since she loves him.
He thinks her family would accept an Englishman
of similar position. He might know how the
Austrian families are obsessed with rank, but I am
sure he did not realise the attitude of the old
families in other respects. I found it hard to swallow
when I first heard of it, I can tell you.'

'What attitude?' I asked.

'First, the rigid way that marriages were
arranged. Titles had to be matched, the dowry had
to be right—everything had to be just so. The only
thing that was not considered was the suitability
of temperament and age of the bride and groom.
To put it brutally, marriages were not made for
happiness. They were made for the matching of
nobility and the production of heirs.'

I shuddered.

'Yes, it's not nice, but it was usually accepted by
the brides without question. They were brought
up to consider marriage in that way. And a girl who
did not want to conform had a very hard time.
She could be sent to a convent to repent her dis-
obedience. The Baroness Steffi's father was a hard
man, so that is what would have happened to her,
and he would have decided how long she was to
stay. There would be no question of her marrying
the man of her choice if she had refused the husband planned for her. She knew she must marry
Feldbach or no one, and that she was unlikely ever
to see your father again. She snatched at her one
chance of fulfilment and happiness. It had to last
her a lifetime.'

I understood, and felt sorry for Steffi. But I could
not understand or forgive my father. It seemed to

me that he had betrayed two women . . . *My father*, who had always been to me the soul of honour and an ideal of goodness and kindness.

'When Steffi guessed she might be having Lord Hilary's child, her marriage to Feldbach was imminent. Marthe said she desperately wanted the child—she may even have intended the pregnancy. But if it had been discovered, she would have been utterly disgraced, and would still not have been allowed to marry your father. Having ruined herself and dishonoured her family, she would not be rewarded for her "sin", as they would have called it. She knew what would be done. Do you?'

I shook my head.

'She would have been put in a convent—*for life*. As soon as she had had her child, it would have been taken away, to be brought up in a foundling home, its parentage never acknowledged. She would never have seen it. She knew her only hope of keeping her child was to pass it off as Feldbach's. She swore Marthe to secrecy, and took the gamble. It worked. And since she had no more children, Adèle became the Baron's heir.'

'How ironical! If the Baron had known . . .'

'I'm not so sure that he didn't. He was not young; and, from what Marthe said, I guessed he was one of those inbred aristocrats.'

I looked at Piers questioningly. I was really very innocent then—such matters had never been discussed in my presence—in fact my aunts would have considered what had been said so far as most indelicate.

'Charlotte, I'm a soldier, and used to blunt speaking. Since you seem not to understand, I must put it plainly. From no fault of his own—simply from inbreeding—Feldbach was physically a poor specimen. It is very likely he could not father children. If so, he probably knew that. For his wife to produce a child in the first year of their marriage would look like a proof of his manhood. He could not afford to disown it, in case he could not give her another.'

I was cross with myself for blushing, but I couldn't help it, it was all so dreadfully intimate. Piers went on talking as if he hadn't noticed.

'It was tragic that Baroness Steffi died so young. When the Baron married again, his will was arranged so that Adèle inherited the bulk of his fortune—perhaps he preferred she should have it, rather than it should be passed on to young Szarvas, who was not popular with him. Marthe said he was genuinely fond of Adèle. Incidentally, he had made no marriage plans for her before he died.'

'So everything went well for Adèle until the Baron died and Baroness Elsa took over?'

'Yes. She did not like the idea of the lawyer handing out just enough money for Adèle's expenses and those of her estates, I should think, for Marthe says she is a greedy woman. Perhaps she thought she ought to have been left more of the money. At all events, it seems she decided the only way she could lay hands on some of it was to marry her son to Adèle as soon as possible.'

'That makes sense,' I answered. 'People will do anything out of greed. Just now I don't care about that—I can only think of Papa—leaving Steffi, coming home and marrying Mama.'

'Don't imagine it was easy for him. He loved her,

but he had to accept the situation. *She* decided to marry Feldbach rather than lose her child and be forced into a life of seclusion. He had no option. But he told her how to contact him if ever she was in need. Then he had to rebuilt his life without her. He met your mother—or perhaps he already knew her—and found he could love again.'

'How is it possible?' I protested. 'It was so soon —not much more than a year! Adèle is less than three years older than I am.'

'Believe me, Charlotte, a year is a long time when a man is lonely. And, can't you see, it is possible to love two people—love them just as dearly, but in different ways? I admit there is nothing like a young man's first love. It is so intense that it can be almost a madness, but it can be replaced by another just as sincere. A man idealises his first love—the second one he understands better, and loves her faults as well as her virtues. I'm not married, but I think that is how a marriage should be. You always thought your father loved your mother. I am sure he did, and I don't suppose either of them regretted their marriage for a single instant.'

The frozen feeling in my heart was thawing. Piers had made me see my father and his situation in a way I myself had not been capable of exploring, but I was still not content.

'But he left me—and rushed to Adèle—without a word . . .'

'Charlotte, he thought he was going to Steffi! How could he explain it to you then? He knew how it would hurt you. He had to find out what the trouble was, and the explanations would have come afterwards.'

'But they didn't. He died because of her,' I retorted stubbornly.

'No! It wasn't her fault—or his. It couldn't be foreseen. My dear child, you're not jealous of Adèle? You had your father for eighteen years. She, I dare say, for as many minutes.'

His words struck home. I hadn't realised it, but it was true. I was jealous of Adèle—jealous that she was Papa's first daughter, born of his first love, and that he had left me and rushed to her when she called. It was selfish and wicked of me. The tears flowed into my eyes and I seized my handkerchief and tried to stop them, turning my face away from Piers, for I felt so ashamed of them, and of my jealousy.

The next moment I felt his arm sliding behind my head, holding me comfortingly against his shoulder. He did not say a word, but just held me gently until my tears subsided, and I scrubbed my cheeks dry. I turned my head towards him again, and he smiled down at me. When I saw the tenderness in his eyes, my heart turned over. Did he really have some affection for me? And, if so, how did he regard me? As a possible sweetheart, or just a likeable young girl not long out of the schoolroom? I could not forget he had years of experience of life—and of women.

'Is that better? I've heard that a good cry helps.'

I managed a shaky laugh. 'I don't know—but you were right. I was jealous. I don't think I am any more. Thank you, Piers, for being so patient and explaining everything to me. Now that I understand, it all seems so different.'

I think I grew up from that moment.

There was a burst of chatter and laughter along the street: someone began to blow a toy trumpet, and went on and on . . .

'Everyone is so noisy!' I complained. 'I didn't realise Vienna was like this until I had to stay in bed.'

He laughed, and drew his arm away. I was sorry to feel it go.

'It isn't, Charlotte, it's *Fasching*! The city goes quite mad, with balls and masquerades and foolery in the streets! It's a shame you're missing it all.'

'Oh, I had quite forgotten. Shall I see any of it?'

'I expect so—it goes on for a long time—until Lent. It started quietly this year, because of Court mourning, but it picked up on the fifteenth, with the Skating Club Ball and the Master Bakers' Ball both on the same night.'

'Did you go to either of them?'

'No. I haven't been to a ball yet—I've been rather busy. But if you get better quickly, I shall hope to do so and be your escort. In fact, you must, or I shall have bought a costume in vain.'

'A costume! You mean you are going to wear fancy dress?'

'Everybody does! The men don't usually wear masks, but the ladies do, which gives them an advantage. They can flirt like mad and disclaim all responsibility.'

'What a good idea! What sort of costume have you got?'

He grinned. 'One that keeps a promise I made you.'

'I don't remember any promise.'

'Didn't I say that one day I'd be a devil?'

'A *devil*! What is it like?'

'Oh—black, tight-fitting, with slashes of red. A black cloak lined with red. A fetching black head-dress with a pair of horns—and a false moustache and a little pointed beard. To finish it off, a splendid rubber pitchfork.'

'Positively satanic! Most suitable! What should I wear?'

'Something from a nursery rhyme—Mary Quite Contrary, I should think!'

'You wretch! I feel more like Jill after tumbling down the hill.'

Later, I was to think that Little Miss Muffet would have been more appropriate. It was certainly an outsize spider—and a wicked web. But at the time I was distracted by Piers dropping a kiss on my forehead as he commanded me to get well. It was just a brotherly sort of kiss, but it set my heart thumping again, which was foolish, as he plainly considered me a silly inexperienced girl who had to be given explanations, comforted, and then cajoled into a good temper.

'And while you are getting better, you can plan your costume. Yes, I like the idea of Mary Quite Contrary—with a gardening apron and basket, a sunbonnet, and perhaps a pair of clogs.'

'*Clogs!*'

Before I could tell him what I thought of that suggestion, he was gone.

The next day I was considered convalescent and allowed to sit up for a short while out of bed, and from then my improvement gathered pace. I was determined to be up and about as soon as possible, not for *Fasching*, though I was not completely insensitive to the delights of the carnival, but because time was passing and we still had not found Adèle. What were Baroness Elsa and her friends doing with her? I guessed that their intention was to isolate her completely among strangers and break her spirit. I thought of the people concerned—a greedy woman, Baroness Elsa; an ambitious and equally greedy woman, Countess Plesch; a greedy and vicious young man, Szarvas—they were capable of doing that. Hovering in the background was Count Palkany. I did not know what interest he could possibly have in the affair, but I felt that he would delight in villainy for villainy's sake. And the longer we took to find Adèle, the worse it would be for her. If they forced her into marriage, it would be irrevocable. Szarvas would have control of her money and they would all have their own way. I was struck with the appalling thought that Adèle would then be of no further use to them; she would be expendable. An accident that was not really an accident—and she would be out of their way.

I found my heart was thumping, and my hands were clammy. I tried to take a grip on myself. An accident that was not really an accident, my mind repeated—and then it struck me like a physical blow. *My father!* Was his accident like that? Did Adèle suspect it—was that why she had said she had killed him? I had dismissed it as a hysterical outburst, but was it? Had he been deliberately killed because she had told him about the way she was being forced into marriage?

Oh, no, it wasn't possible! Now I was being the hysterical one. No one could consider that a reason for murder. Whatever action my father might have been able to take, all they needed to do to counteract it was what they had been doing successfully all the time—to insist that they had no plans for Adèle's marriage, that it was a silly obsession existing only in her brain. My illness had weakened my powers of reasoning and made me fearful; it was high time I pulled myself together.

Then Piers came with the first piece of good news. He had discovered the name and address of Adèle's lawyer.

'That is wonderful!' I exclaimed. 'When can you take me to see him?'

'Gently, Charlotte! You're rushing your fences again! If you do go to see him, what on earth are you going to say? What excuse can you produce?'

'*Excuse?* I don't need an excuse! I shall simply ask him if he knows where she is. I want to see her—she is not at the Palace, and I find it strange that no one will tell me where she has gone. As her lawyer, I expect him to know her whereabouts. If he doesn't, I hope I shall give him something to think about—and to act on!'

'Well, that's one method of attack, and it's probably your best one. But be very careful. Don't make any accusations about Baroness Feldbach —that would antagonise a lawyer at once, and you'd get no co-operation from him.'

I considered that carefully. 'Yes, you are probably right. My angle must be that I want to see her again before I leave Vienna, nothing more.'

Once I had agreed to that, Piers said he would take me as soon as I was fit and an appointment could be arranged.

'I'm fit now, Piers! Please get me an appointment as soon as you can? Poor Adèle, it's been so long, she'll think we have deserted her.'

Piers made an appointment and in due course called for me in a carriage. When I walked out of the house, I found I was not quite as strong as I thought, but still a little shaky. However, I successfully concealed this.

The lawyer's office was in an attractive building in the old quarter. It was plainly a family firm of such long standing that it had not been considered necessary to move to a more fashionable district. When we were shown into Herr Mayer's presence, I thought he might as well have been the founder. He was not merely elderly, he was positively venerable, with bigger sidewhiskers than the Emperor; he was a symphony in shades of grey, from the silver of his hair to the pearl of his cravat and the darker shade of his buttoned-up tail-coat.

He greeted me with profound courtesy and asked in what way he could serve me. If he had any visions of an expensive lawsuit, he was swiftly disillusioned.

'I must apologise for intruding on your valuable time, Herr Mayer,' I said. 'I have come to trouble you for a little information.'

He looked at me questioningly and said nothing. Piers coughed—warningly, I thought.

'As Baroness Adèle Phönix's lawyer, I hope you will be able to put me in touch with her.'

His look became inscrutable. It seemed it was not correct to ask a lawyer for information.

'May I know why you wish to be in touch?' he asked slowly.

'My father was a friend of her family,' I said rashly. I had to establish myself somehow, and went on, 'When I came here from England, I contacted the Baroness and paid a call on her in the Phoenix Palace. I discovered she had been ill and was not fully recovered, but she asked me to visit her again. Now I find she has left the Palace. Baroness Feldbach is not there either, and the servants will not tell me where they have gone.'

'Servants, Lady Charlotte, are paid to be discreet. No doubt they had their instructions.'

'I am sure they did. That is why I have come to you. As her lawyer, you must know where she is.'

'Not necessarily, Lady Charlotte. My clients do not expect to inform me of all their comings and goings.'

'Of course not, but the Baroness Adèle is surely a special case? She is an orphan, and still a minor. And she has been ill. I would imagine that you have a close contact with her and the Baroness Feldbach. If not, you are hardly taking full care of her interests.'

'Charlotte!'

I felt Piers's restraining hand on my arm, but ignored it, for I could see that my questioning of Herr Mayer's efficiency in professional matters had touched him on a tender spot.

'*Gnädiges Fräulein!*' he said, reproach in look and voice. 'I am most concerned over the Baroness's interests. Of course I know where she is.'

'Then perhaps you would be so kind as to tell me?' I said sweetly. 'Then I need take up no more of your time.'

'It is not as simple as that, *gnädiges Fräulein*. The family do not wish her whereabouts to be known, for she needs rest. She is not to be troubled in any way.'

'Herr Mayer, I am not going to trouble her. I simply want to know where she is. If I call, and she is not well enough to see me, she will at least know I have paid her the courtesy.'

He sat behind his desk like a potentate and considered this. I sat opposite him, pondering my next tactic.

'Lady Charlotte, if you wish, I shall forward a letter to her.'

'Thank you, but I do not wish that, Herr Mayer. A letter is not the same thing at all. If she is in hospital, I would want to enquire after her, and leave some suitable gift.'

For the moment he looked disconcerted. 'Why do you suggest she may be in hospital?'

'Because I know she has been ill. *Is* she in hospital?'

There was a long pause. To get anything out of him was like prising open an oyster.

'Yes—and no.'

'Just what does that mean?'

'It means—that she is having special care.'

'So I would hope—but where?'

I turned on him my most winning smile. Perhaps being feminine and suppliant would be more effective.

'Of course you wish to spare her from anything that may slow down her recovery,' I went on. 'But, Herr Mayer, so do I. It would please her to see me, or, if she is not well enough, to know that I am thinking of her and care about her. You would be doing us both a great kindness if you gave me the address. I may just call and leave her some flowers.'

He sat stroking his chin.

'I am so upset about her,' I said, and brought out my handkerchief to dab at my eyes.

'Ah, yes, to be sure. Do not distress yourself, *gnädiges Fräulein*. If—and I say *if*—I were to give you the address, you realise it would be in the utmost confidence?'

'Naturally. Oh, will you?'

'*If* I do, you will promise not to reveal it to anyone else?'

'Of course—besides, I hardly know anyone here, the occasion would not arise . . .'

'Very well. This is the place.'

He wrote in a slow, elegant hand on a sheet of paper and handed it to me. I glanced at it—the name meant nothing—folded it, and tucked it into my purse.

'I cannot thank you enough, Herr Mayer.'

He got up, and we said our formal goodbyes. Then, on impulse, I turned back as he showed me to the door.

'Herr Mayer, would you be so good as to give me one of your cards? You have been so kind—and discreet—that I should like to recommend you if an occasion arose.'

'If you wish, Lady Charlotte.'

He managed to convey in his slight reluctance that he never needed an extra client and that my suggestion was lowering to his high professional status, but he went to his desk, found a card and gave it to me. I thanked him again, and we left.

Back in the carriage, Piers gave a great gusty sigh and shook his head at me.

'Charlotte, you are incorrigible! I did not dare to interfere in case I made matters worse. You are an actress, a little liar, and an absolute minx! You blackmailed and bullied and wheedled that address out of the poor man!'

'Thank you for your compliments, Piers. Poor man, indeed! He's old and hidebound, and not fit to handle the affairs of someone like Adèle who needs protection.'

'You should be grateful for his age! A younger man might have seen through your crocodile tears and not given in to you!'

'You mustn't judge everyone by yourself, Piers —just because you can read me all too well and are hard-hearted into the bargain.'

'Hard-hearted, am I? Never mind. Now you have the address, where is Adèle?'

I fished the paper out of my purse and gave it to him. 'It must be a private nursing-home.'

He looked at the paper long and hard, making no movement except that caused by the swaying of the carriage, his face fixed and serious, sitting as if petrified. I could not understand it, but as the seconds passed I felt all at once full of apprehension, gripped by an unreasoning fear, and I could not bear his silence.

'What is it, Piers?' I said at last.

'Clinic Édouard Dietrich,' he read slowly. 'I saw an advertisement for it in the paper only a few days ago. It opened quite recently.'

'Well? A new nursing-home. She may get better, more modern, treatment there.'

'Oh, she will get treatment,' he replied, but his face and voice were grim. 'And modern, certainly. But it is not a hospital or a nursing-home in that sense.'

'What is it, then?'

'The Clinic Édouard Dietrich is a private lunatic asylum.'

CHAPTER NINE

I WAS AGHAST, horrified. 'Piers, are you sure?'

'Quite sure. Vienna has thrown up recently a number of doctors who are specialising in mental disturbances, trying to trace their origins in the patients' past experiences, hoping to cure them by uncovering the causes. I dare say some of them are perfectly genuine, and in time their theories may be proved to have some basis. But at the moment the way is clear for anyone who has some sort of medical qualification to open up a clinic, and these theories are so new that no layman can be sure of sorting out the genuine from the charlatan. I have heard of Dietrich; I don't say he's a quack, but he is a doctor who has given up medicine.'

'How *can* she be in such a place!' I cried. 'Adèle is sane, nervous, but as sane as you or I . . .'

'Perhaps Dr Dietrich was easily convinced that Adèle is unbalanced. He lives too grandly for a doctor: perhaps he is unscrupulous enough to take money when no treatment is needed.'

'Piers, you mean—he would keep her there . . . just because Baroness Elsa paid him to?'

'I think we have underestimated Baroness Elsa. Or perhaps she has been advised by someone cleverer than she is. If Adèle won't agree to the marriage, the next best thing is to have her committed as insane. I don't know, but it might then be possible to get control of her money, or more of it

than at present. Herr Mayer would have to be
convinced, of course. That should be easy for them.
Adèle, telling one story, driven hysterical by being
kept in such a place, and her stepmother quietly
telling another tale and insisting she is imagining
the whole thing.'

I was cold and trembling. 'You mean they would
leave her there—for *ever*?'

'No,' he said, in a voice like steel. 'A few years
should be enough. And we can look on the bright
side. They may simply be blackmailing her—she
can come out if she agrees to marry. If she changes
her mind, she goes back in again.'

'Yes,' I said. 'That is what Adèle told me. She
said that she would be sent somewhere worse. This
is what they meant.'

I found I was sobbing—hard, dry, tearless sobs.

Piers's hands gripped my arms firmly. 'Charlotte,
it may not be like that. I may have got the wrong
impression, imagined it . . .'

'You are not the one who imagines things! Now
that we know where she is, we must go and get her
out of there at once.' I struggled to control myself.

'No!' he said, and it was a command. 'That's
quite impossible. You cannot go to a private clinic
and demand the release of a patient over whom you
have no rights. To go there at all at present would
alert Baroness Elsa. And I'm quite sure she will
have given Dietrich his instructions. We would get
nowhere.'

'Piers, we can't just leave her there!' I said
frantically. 'We must . . .'

'Of course we must get her out, but it needs to be
considered carefully. At the moment, I cannot see

any way they could be persuaded to give her up
—and we have no legal rights.'

'Nor, it seems, has she! Then there's only one
thing to do—we must persuade Herr Mayer to get
her out. As her lawyer . . .'

'As her lawyer, he should have some power, but
can you see him using it? He was so reluctant to tell
you where she is, that I expect he considers a case of
lunacy among his clients a disgrace and a scandal.
And he must have been convinced she needs to be
there. My impression is that he would agree to her
release only if she were going to be kept under strict
supervision at home. That would suit Baroness
Feldbach. Adèle once having been accepted by the
asylum, she will have every excuse for keeping her
more or less a prisoner until she does exactly what is
wanted.'

I felt stunned, and numb with the horror of it. To
think of Adèle in an asylum—she had already been
there two or three weeks—in her delicate state of
health it might be enough to make her unbalanced
in fact. I just stared at Piers.

'Charlotte, don't look at me like that! We'll find a
way, but there's nothing we can do today. We must
tread very carefully. I must look into the legal
aspects, for a start.'

'Thank you very much!' I flared at him. 'I suppose I should be grateful that you at least acknowl-
edge that she is being badly treated. So she is to be
left in an asylum, among lunatics, treated like a
lunatic, while you look into the legal aspects! If she
knew, I'm sure it would be a comfort to her!'

'Charlotte, be fair! No one can do anything active
at present. Any move, even going to the clinic and

leaving a message, would put the stepmother on her guard. The very fact that matters have reached this stage means we must be particularly careful.'

I had to agree with the logic of that.

He went on, 'You are still convalescent, so please be a good girl, stop worrying and leave this to me.'

A good girl! I could have hit him. Why did he persistently treat me like a child? So he was going to bring his man's brain to bear on Adèle's problem? Well, I should put my feeble woman's brain to work, and we should see who came up the quicker with a feasible plan.

For the rest of the day I was actively thinking about Adèle. When I went to bed, I was exploring an idea that had just come to me; and before I went to sleep I had a plan fully formed in my mind. One couldn't cover everything, of course. There were far too many uncertainties and imponderables, but an attempt had to be made to release her. If it failed, everything would turn on whether Piers's slower, legal methods could be effective. I only hoped my plan might succeed by its very simplicity.

I could not safely do everything alone. And I could not call on Piers, for he would immediately veto the whole idea. It had to be Marthe and Gottlieb; and this form one angle was good, because Adèle had confidence in them.

When Lady Bellanger went out on her social round—regretfully accepting my decision that I was not fit enough to go with her—I took a cab and went to Marthe's room. This time I knew exactly where it was, and was able to scuttle up there without being accosted or having my purse snatched. And I was lucky; Marthe was alone.

I told her where Adèle was, and she was as shocked as I had been. I cut short her piteous protests and said firmly, 'Don't worry, Marthe. We are going to get her out.'

'Is it possible?'

'I hope so. I have a plan, and I am going to do my best. But I need your help, for if it works and Baroness Adèle is able to walk out of that place, you must be waiting—you and Gottlieb—to take her to safety in the British Embassy.'

I told her what I intended to do. With a peasant's respect for authority—in this case the dreaded powers of the officials of an asylum—she was at once fearful and uncertain.

'Marthe, you have nothing to worry about,' I insisted. 'It is my responsibility. You love your mistress and she needs you. It isn't difficult. All you have to do is to be waiting with Gottlieb and the cab. Get her to the Embassy, ask for Captain Talbot, and do not leave her until he comes. You can do that, can't you?'

She pulled herself together. 'Yes, milady. We'll do it.'

'Very well. I'll call for you this evening.'

The day passed very slowly for me, and anticipation made me nervous. It was a risky scheme; I could be certain of nothing; yet I had to try it. I could not leave Adèle there, thinking I had deserted her, believing she was condemned to remain for ever at the mercy of that infamous quartet.

While the household was dressing for dinner, I got ready. Over my dark day dress I put a warm cloak, and tucked up my hair under my fur hat, which I had liberally swathed with veiling. I put what I needed in the little purse in the lining of my muff, and it was done. I slipped out of the house.

It did not occur to me that it would be difficult to get a cab. At *Fasching*, all were busy collecting people to take them to balls and suppers and celebrations. I ranged up and down in the slush of the pavement, my feet getting frozen in my thin boots, trying not to panic as the minutes passed. There was no fixed time, I told myself, but I knew that getting a cab would grow more and more difficult as the evening wore on. And then luck was with me. A cab came clopping along, and as I waved frantically at it, the cabbie drew his horse to a stop.

'Well, *Fräulein*, you're not dressed for *Fasching*! Some emergency, is it? Where do you want to go?'

I told him, and saw him looking doubtful—he thought it was not going to be a profitable fare, after all.

'But that's the first call,' I went on quickly. 'I must pick up an old couple there. Then we must go to a private clinic. I want you to wait for someone to come out. I'll pay you well, for it's important.'

I took out a gold coin and put it in his hand. 'Take that in advance. Do as I ask, and you won't lose by it.'

'Oh, that will suit me, *Fräulein*. I don't mind waiting as long as I get paid.'

I got in and the cab rattled off. Soon we passed a flower-seller sheltering in an archway; I stopped the cab, got out and bought a handsome bunch. Then we went on. At the building where Marthe was staying, the cabbie pulled up and helped me out. I tried to hurry upstairs—oh, those stairs! I was still not strong, and they winded me. Marthe and Gottlieb were waiting, we went down at once, and I gave the cabbie the address of the clinic.

We sat there in the cab. I was tense, the old folks were nervous.

'I hope you know what you're doing, *Fräulein*,' said Gottlieb.

'I know,' I replied. 'All you have to do is wait —wait until you see me or Baroness Adèle. If anything goes wrong, I shall come out, but for her sake you had better say your prayers that my plan succeeds.'

The winter dark had closed down on the city. The street lamps were alight, and we passed people going to their particular revels. There were men in evening dress, but many more were in costume. Harlequins, pirates, jesters, Turkish pashas, Chinese mandarins—these were commonplace; in other disguises, imagination had run riot. As for the toilettes of the ladies, they were even more fantastic. And whether she was a Watteau shepherdess, a vivid butterfly or a fairy-tale princess, every lady wore a mask—not a simple black domino, but a creation of satin and spangles, some with ribbon streamers, some with crests of feathers. It was my first glimpse of *Fasching*, and if my business had not been so serious, I would have been fascinated enough to drive round the streets for hours looking at the revellers. But, tonight, Carnival was not for me.

Marthe and Gottlieb received the rest of their instructions. The clinic was in a smart street that led into the Ring. I told the cabbie to stop some little distance from the house, and wait. Gottlieb was to station himself on the pavement near by; Marthe could wait in the cab until—I hoped—Adèle appeared. They were to drive off with her at once.

'But what about you, milady?' Marthe asked.

'I shall look after myself. It is most important to get the Baroness away *at once*! You must wait, it doesn't matter how long, until one of us comes.'

They understood. I took my courage in both hands, got out, and walked quickly up to the door of the clinic.

It looked very respectable: a good entrance, a neat brass plate beside it. The outer door was open, but I had to knock to be admitted through the inner one. The maid only half opened the door, but I walked arrogantly past into a long and narrow hall. She hurried after me, rather flustered, and prepared to take the flowers I was holding, asking to whom they were to be given. But I kept them in my hand.

'I should like to see the Baroness Phönix,' I told her.

'The Baroness Phönix?' She looked startled. '*Fräulein*, she is not allowed visitors.'

'Not allowed visitors?' I repeated. 'But she is not seriously ill. I have come especially to see her.'

'I'm sorry, *Fräulein*, those are my instructions.'

She was a young girl, and I had hoped to overawe her, but in spite of her nervousness it was not so easy.

'Then will you please find someone who gives you your instructions,' I said coolly.

'You are only wasting your time, *Fräulein*. It is not allowed.'

As she spoke, a door at the lower end of the hall opened and an older woman came towards us. 'What is the matter?' she asked.

As she came into the light of the lamp, it seemed to me that I had seen her before. Yet I could not think that I had met her, and in any case why should I remember her, for her appearance was unremarkable. She was a nicely dressed, rather ordinary looking middle-aged woman.

'It's about the Baroness Phönix, Frau Dietrich,' the maid explained. So this was the wife of the doctor in charge! 'This lady wishes to see her.'

'You know she is not allowed visitors,' the older woman said, too firmly for my liking.

'Yes, I told the lady so.'

'Frau Dietrich!' I said. 'I am very pleased to meet you. May I introduce myself? I am Lady Charlotte Brantham, here on a brief visit from England. I have had considerable difficulty in finding the Baroness—surely you will not refuse me a few minutes with her?'

'It is the rule. How did you know she was here?'

'That is why I think you may let me see her. I know her lawyer, Herr Mayer.' From inside my muff, I brought out his card. 'He told me the circumstances, and said that if I produced his card you would relax the rule and let me see her, so that I shall not have to go back to England without saying goodbye.'

'Herr Mayer said that?'

'Yes,' I lied boldly.

'And what did he tell you?'

'That she is suffering from some slight delusion, but is not violent. That is correct?'

'Up to a point, yes.'

I practically held the card under her nose. My heart was going pit-a-pat, but I forced myself to look calm and to keep my voice steady. 'So, with Herr Mayer's recommendation, you will let me see her?'

The woman did not at once say 'No'. I prayed that my bluff would succeed. If it failed, there was nothing I could do.

'Shall I go and ask Dr Dietrich?' the maid suggested.

Perhaps Frau Dietrich resented the implication that she had not enough authority. Whatever it was, something goaded her into a decision.

'It is not necessary,' she snapped at the maid. Then she turned back to me. 'You may have a few minutes with her. But the visit must be brief, and cannot be repeated.'

'I quite understand. I simply wish to say goodbye,' I replied.

'Follow me.'

That's the first hurdle, I said to myself, as we went down the hall and began to mount the stairs. Next, I must be alone with Adèle. What shall I do if Frau Dietrich insists on staying with us like a wardress? She marched stiffly before me. Up one flight—up two flights—and still I had seen no one else. How many resident patients did the doctor have? I wondered. And were they always so quiet? This was mercifully unlike my idea of a lunatic asylum. The place was furnished to look like an upper-class private house.

Half-way along the corridor, the woman stopped. From her pocket she brought out a bunch of keys, unlocked the door, and stepped in first.

'Baroness, you have a visitor,' she said.

Adèle was sunk in an armchair at the end of the room. She looked up sharply, and there was fear in her face. I moved forward and spoke her name, thankful to see she did not look markedly more ill than when I had last seen her. She struggled to her feet and came towards me, hands outstretched. I dropped the flowers on the top of a chest and took her in my arms.

'Gently!' I whispered in her ear. 'Keep calm. Just say you're glad to see me.'

'Charlotte! Charlotte!' she gasped. 'Oh—I am glad—I am so glad to see you!'

'Let us sit down,' I said. 'I can't stay long.'

Frau Dietrich, I noticed, was examining the flowers. Satisfied that there was no message hidden in them, she said to me, 'I'll leave you for a few minutes. I must lock the door, for the security of the patient. A nurse will come and let you out when you have had your time.'

Exactly what I wanted, I thought. She went out and locked the door behind her. Adèle was sobbing in my arms.

'I thought you had . . . I was locked up here . . . I didn't know what they would do!' She was almost incoherent.

'Adèle, listen carefully—we've got very little time.' I said firmly. 'You want to get out of here, don't you? Then it has to be *now*.'

'*Now?*'

The plan that had come to me the previous night was simple. It had historical precedents, which was probably why I had thought of it; and one or two of them had succeeded. It was simply a case of our changing identities.

'Yes, Adèle. You have got to leave here instead of me.'

Already I was taking off my hat and cloak. I thanked heaven that Adèle was dressed, and not in bed, and that she was wearing a dark gown.

'Put these on. We must tuck up all your hair under the hat, so that the different colour will not be noticed. Now, listen.'

As I arranged the hat, I went on talking. 'When the nurse comes, you will walk out of the room as if you were me. Turn left and go down the corridor to the stairs. There are two flights, and then you will be in the hall. If you can't open the inner door, there will be a maid—let her do it. You can be using your handkerchief so that she won't see too much of your face. Outside, Marthe and Gottlieb will be waiting. They will take you to my Embassy. They know what to do.'

'Charlotte, I can't! Someone will see me . . . They'll never let me out!'

'Adèle, if you want to escape, this is the only way! We look alike . . . You can walk, can't you, enough to get out of the house?'

'I—I think so . . .'

'You *must*!' I was taking off her shawl and putting my cloak about her. 'Now you know what to do—there are two flights of stairs, just *walk out*, don't run. If anyone speak to you, take no notice. Pretend to be crying. As soon as you are outside, Marthe and Gottlieb will be with you.'

'Oh, Charlotte, I'll try! But what about you?'

'Don't worry about me. I'm not their patient

—they can't keep me! Here's my muff. Let me look at you. Yes, we're really very much alike. You can do it, if you keep your head.'

I was terribly afraid she would have a nervous collapse, become hysterical, or simply lack the courage to carry out my scheme. But a core of strength had survived in her through all the evil treatment, and her spirit was not broken, although she was physically very weak.

'I'll try. I'll do it,' she said.

'Good!' I took up her shawl and draped it over my head and shoulders. 'Now I'm going to sit in your chair,' I told her. 'Take the other and sit beside me, and when the nurse comes in, get up and kiss me goodbye. You will be able to keep your back to her most of the time.' I adjusted the veiling on the hat a little lower. 'Just nod and go straight out.'

We sat down, close to each other, and I held her hand in mine. I think we were both trembling.

'I can't believe it!' she whispered. 'I can't believe I'll get out . . .'

'You *will*,' I said. 'I got in—I believe that was harder!'

She managed a smile at my poor joke.

'You'll be all right,' I emphasised.

We heard the key rattle in the lock. She gripped my hand frantically. I hoped it would look as if I were gripping hers.

'Kiss me now,' I murmured, as the door opened behind me.

She got up, put her arms round me and kissed me.

'Good luck!' I whispered.

She turned and walked out, fumbling in my muff, head down.

'Well, you're lucky!' said a voice. 'I didn't think you were allowed visitors.'

I pulled the shawl round me, thankful that the lamplight was weak and that I was sitting in shadow, and hunched myself in my chair, pretending to be crying.

'Oh, so we're not talking! You should be grateful. Stop snivelling, and when your supper comes, eat it up. Oh, flowers, eh? But you're not allowed vases, they're breakable. I'll have them.'

I heard the door being shut and locked, and I was alone.

Adèle—Adèle! I prayed. Let her find enough strength, enough cunning to manage it. How much start did she have? She might have reached the head of the stairs before the nurse locked this door. Let her not meet anyone. I sat there, counting her paces, counting the stairs, allowing time for her weakness—would that be one flight? If she were discovered, would I hear anything? How shall I know if she has escaped? If she were found out, surely they would bring her back here? They would want to find me, of course. As long as I was left here undisturbed, couldn't I assume that the switch of identities had not been discovered? Two flights now? But I couldn't know, they might be cunning enough to let me think we had succeeded while Adèle was being locked up somewhere else. Was she in the hall by now? Was she leaving the house? Was Marthe taking her in her arms, was Gottlieb helping her into the cab? Please God, let them all be rattling off to the Embassy. Please God . . .

Minutes passed. The house was silent, although the street noises penetrated very faintly. I could not know what had happened. I was locked in, and the sense of imprisonment began to weigh on me. I got up, went to the window and parted the curtains. Outside—bars and blackness. The room must be at the back of the house; it probably overlooked a courtyard between other buildings. The room was comfortably furnished, but the bed was bolted to the floor. A cupboard and a chest of drawers were also immovable. I went back to the chair. There was nothing to be done.

The wait seemed interminable, and yet my watch told me it was not many minutes. Then the key rattled in the lock again, the door opened and a young maid came in with a tray which she set down on a small table near to me. I ignored her, not daring to turn my head, for the longer I could keep up my imposture the better, but I saw her from out of the corner of my eye. She did not look at me, but put down the tray and went straight out. I guessed the nurse who had come in before, and whom I believed from her voice to be an older woman, was opening doors and standing guard while the suppers were delivered.

If our plan had succeeded, I would probably be left until the maid came to collect the tray. Three books were on the table, but I certainly could not settle to reading. I suddenly realised that I had missed dinner, and was hungry. With a slightly hysterical giggle, I thought, Well, here's a supper going begging!

It was not what I would have had at Lady Bellanger's. It was not unwholesome, but was definitely not *haute cuisine*. A bowl of thin meat stew with dumplings and potatoes, a chunk of bread, no butter, a piece of cheese and a slice of plain cake. A very starchy meal, but it would be filling. I looked closer at the tray—there were two spoons, not a knife or fork. I ate most of the supper nevertheless.

Silence and inactivity were getting on my nerves. I decided that by now either Adèle was safe, or my plan had failed completely and someone was playing cat and mouse with me. When the door was opened again I should get up, show myself, and demand to leave.

At last the key was clattered and turned. As the door opened, I stood up, and letting the shawl fall from my head, stepped out of the shadow into the lamplight. The young maid glanced at me—gasped —stared—and let out a cry of surprise. Instantly an older woman in nurse's uniform appeared in the doorway. She took one look at me, exclaimed, *'Mein Gott!'*, caught the maid by the arm and dragged her outside. Her reaction and movements were so swift that I had no time to say a word before the door was shut and locked yet again.

That was something I had not expected. I thought an explanation would be demanded, that I would then tell the nurse she could not keep me there, and march out, leaving her confounded. She had been too quick for me; she was probably used to anticipating difficult or unruly patients. So I must wait a little longer. She would return with Frau Dietrich, or perhaps even the doctor himself.

I was right in that guess. The next time the door opened, it seemed to admit a positive crowd, who resolved themselves into two nurses, Frau Dietrich and a middle-aged man, whom I suddenly recognised.

Seeing him with Frau Dietrich, the memory flooded back: that broad large-featured face with sidewhiskers and moustache, the wide thin-lipped mouth, the black frock-coat with pince-nez clipped to the lapel—I had last seen them opposite his nondescript wife at a dining table on the Orient Express!

'So!' he said commandingly. 'What is this? Where is the Baroness Phönix?'

'She is out of your asylum, Dr Dietrich,' I told him firmly. 'And so she should be—she is no madder than you or I.'

'So you decided to take her place?'

His voice was smooth, but it had an unpleasant edge nevertheless.

'It seemed a good idea. It worked, too. And now I will go.'

'Oh, please do not rush away,' he said with heavy irony. 'Since the Baroness has gone, I really feel you should stay and explain her absence to the Baroness Feldbach.'

'That is your job!' I said bluntly. 'You were in charge of her. As paid jailer, it is your responsibility.'

His eyes narrowed, and a muscle in his jaw twitched. 'Do not be arrogant with me, Lady Charlotte. I insist that you stay.'

'You cannot keep me here,' I said shortly, and moved towards the door, but for all my assumed confidence I was beginning to feel more than a little nervous. I had good reason to be; I had taken only three steps when the two nurses pounced on me, each seizing an arm. I tried to throw them off, but they just gripped me the harder.

I was still weak from my illness—they were strong and knew what they were doing. Still, I struggled. I fought them with all my strength, and I kicked into the bargain, for this was no occasion for ladylike behaviour. Dr Dietrich intended to keep me here for the time being, but I had no wish to stay while he summoned Baroness Elsa, who would probably arrive with the rest of her contingent.

My struggles were short-lived, but not because I had exhausted my strength. On seeing me doing my best to fight off his wardresses, Dr Dietrich made a sign to his wife, who had been standing in the background. She was holding something; she made a couple of swift movements, and then came towards me. I smelt a sweet sickly aroma—there was a pad in her hand—a pad which she placed firmly over my nose and mouth. I shook my head to and fro, but with the two nurses holding me it was not difficult for her to keep the pad in place. I struggled and gasped, but could not avoid the revolting odour of the chloroform. Then my eyes began to dazzle, my head began to swim, my legs collapsed under me, and I fell into a black pit of unconsciousness.

How long I was out, I do not know. My senses returned gradually, my head was aching as well as swimming, I felt sick, and my mouth had a beastly taste. Opening my eyes, I realised that I was still in Adèle's room, lying on the bed. When I attempted to move, to my horror I found that I was paralysed. Did chloroform do *that*? Try as I might, my legs and arms would not move, there was a tightness across my chest and my whole body felt rigid. Yet there was sensation—I could flex my muscles.

And then the horror really overwhelmed me. It was the most ghastly moment I had ever experienced, to know I was totally impotent, completely at the mercy of whoever had done this to me.

I was bound from head to foot in a lunatic's straitjacket.

CHAPTER TEN

I THINK I screamed, just one scream, and then stopped. I did not flatter myself that anyone would take any notice, so I might as well keep what shreds of dignity remained to me. They weren't much, with my hair falling down and my body bound up like a sausage. My every instinct cried out to me to struggle, to try to free myself, but reason told me I would only be wasting my strength. I was strapped in most ingeniously, even my hands were covered by the flaps of the coarse canvas sleeves, my arms secured across my chest. All I could do was to wait, and pray for release.

There was plenty to think about. Not Adèle—I was now confident that she was safe in the Embassy. My thoughts, I regret to admit, were entirely selfish ones. What did the doctor hope to do with me? Was he keeping me as a kind of hostage against the loss of his real prisoner? When the Baroness Feldbach came, what would she do? She must see that she could not keep me in custody, even if she had any reason for so doing.

I comforted myself with the knowledge that my absence, hours ago, from the dinner table would have caused the Bellangers to make enquiries. Their logical reaction would be to ask Piers at the Embassy whether he had seen me. As soon as Adéle appeared, he would know where I had been, and would guess I had been detained in the clinic.

So I really had nothing to worry about—Piers would come here, and having been alerted by Adèle, would arrive, I expected, with police and a search-warrant. That might take a little time to get, especially at night, during *Fasching*, but Piers would do it, I was certain. It was a reassuring thought. But it would not have been so reassuring had I realised that other people, besides me, were capable of working that out.

Piers—Piers—he would rescue me—he must rescue me! How wrong I had been about him. He wasn't stuffy at all, he was everything a man should be, and I was hopelessly in love with him. It was only now, when I needed him so badly, that I saw how empty life would be without him when I was back in England, living with one or other of the aunts; how I would long for one of his outrageous remarks, how I would yearn to see him looking at me with that ironic sparkle in his clear grey eyes. I told myself to stop being a fool. There was no point in regretting the future in England when I was bound hand and foot in Vienna.

Footsteps sounded in the corridor, and Dr Dietrich entered the room, his wife behind him. He came and stood by the bed, looking down at me.

'So you are conscious,' he said. 'What do you think I shall do with you, you foolish little English-woman?'

'You had better let me go, at once!' I retorted. 'You should know you cannot keep one of Her Majesty's subjects a prisoner.'

He smiled and nodded. 'Quite so. It would be bad for my reputation, would it not? So I shall get rid of you as soon as possible.'

For a dreadful moment I thought he was going to kill me. He'd make it look like another of those Viennese suicides . . .

Frau Dietrich moved over to me. 'Come along.'

She took me by the shoulders, and trussed up as I was, I tried to avoid her. The attempted movement raised such a wave of nausea in me that I retched. If she had not anticipated me and seized a bowl from the table, I would have been sick over her. I wish I had. It was she who had given me the beastly chloroform. When I had finished, she went to the door. The next think I knew, the two nurses had come in with a stretcher, and they were heaving me on to it.

'You can't do this! Let me go!' I gasped.

'She may decide to scream,' remarked Frau Dietrich, and prising open my jaws, she slipped a kind of hard rubber bar between them and fastened it behind my head. At once I felt frantic. If I were to be sick again, I would choke. Thank goodness the doctor had the sense to think of this.

'It's not nice, the gag, is it?' he said chattily. 'Will you promise not to scream? At the first sign, it will go in again, whether you feel sick or not. If you agree to be quiet, nod your head.'

I nodded. I couldn't risk that dreadful thing. Reluctantly, I thought, Frau Dietrich removed it.

Now I was covered up on the stretcher, which the nurses lifted between them. Strength must have been one of their main qualifications; they made very little of the awkward job of carrying me down two flights of stairs and along the hall. Outside in the street, not much was happening—the few drunken revellers took little notice of the waiting ambulance cab and the stretcher case that was carried out to it.

'Goodbye, *Fräulein*,' said Dr Dietrich as I was lifted in. 'I hope we do not meet again.'

Frau Dietrich and the nurses joined me inside the ambulance, the door was shut, and the vehicle creaked its way along the street. I had no idea where I was going. At least, I thought, death was surely not imminent? To tip me into the Danube in a straightjacket would be obvious murder, and straitjackets are not a common article in most households.

Nobody said a word, and we jerked and jolted and creaked along in darkness for some time. Then we stopped, paused, I felt the cab turn as we moved again and went a little further. Now I could hear the sound of the wheels echoing almost as if we were in a tunnel. We stopped again.

The door of the ambulance was opened from outside, and the nurses got out. Frau Dietrich tied a white linen cloth round my head and pulled it partly over my face.

'You've pretended to be the Baroness once, so you can do it again,' she said to me. Then she supervised as the stretcher was pulled out of the ambulance.

Lying on my back, all I could see at first was that I was in a place of vast, enclosed, echoing darkness. Someone lit a lamp, and then another, and I re-alised that I was in the great hall of the Phoenix Palace. Two flunkeys, sleepy-eyed and unshaven, in rumpled livery, came up and lifted the stretcher. They were clumsy, unused to managing it, but the stairs were wide and shallow and they carried me up without too much difficulty, Frau Dietrich and one of the nurses following them.

We turned right instead of left at the head of the staircase, and into a salon I had not seen. Inside, Baroness Elsa, wrapped in a dressing-robe, was waiting. The footman took me through to an inside room and set the stretcher on the floor. Frau Dietrich and the nurse lifted me on to the bed; the footmen picked up the stretcher and left the room. The Baroness shut and locked the door.

Frau Dietrich spoke to me first. 'Your comfort and your amount of freedom depend on you. You will be locked in, and you cannot get out of this room any more than you could from the clinic. If you behave yourself—that is, if you keep quiet and make no fuss—you can come out of the jacket. If you start screaming and shouting and banging on windows or doors, you will be strapped up, or chloroformed, or both. Do you understand?'

'Yes.'

'Are you going to behave and do as you are told?'

'Yes.'

I could see that at present they had so much the upper hand that I might as well settle for limited freedom on their terms. As Frau Dietrich removed the covering blanket and began to unstrap me, I addressed the Baroness.

'How long do you intend to keep me here? It will do you no good—I shall soon be traced.'

The Baroness did not answer, and Frau Dietrich remarked with satisfaction, 'Well, you'll not be found at the clinic.'

'You'll stay until we've decided what to do with you,' said the Baroness.

I noticed that she said 'we', not 'I'.

'And meanwhile the servants are to think that I am Adèle?'

'It is simpler that way.'

'I would hardly have thought so!'

'Mind your own business,' said Frau Dietrich. 'You're not here to argue.'

'I really am sorry for your patients,' I remarked.

She paused long enough from her unbuckling to strike me a sharp blow across the face with her open hand. 'Arrogant bitch!' she said coldly.

I was stiff and cramped, and as the straitjacket came off I felt my half-numbed limbs protesting when the blood began to flow more freely, as I tried to move and rub them. Frau Dietrich rolled it up.

'This is Adèle's room,' the Baroness said to me. 'If you're sensible, you'll go to sleep for the rest of the night. You won't be disturbed until morning.'

Frau Dietrich went out with her, and the door was locked.

Suddenly I found that I was very tired, almost too tired to take stock of my situation. The Baroness was probably right: since I was not at the clinic, it was unlikely that anyone would come here for me yet. I was sure they would come. To Piers, it would be the logical place, but he might not find it easy to get the right to enter a private house, and such an important one, with no hard evidence that I was here. And the Baroness was waiting to discuss with her cronies before deciding what to do with me.

I looked round the room for toilet necessities, and found that they have been provided. I took off my dress. The water in the jug on the washstand was cold, but it was refreshing to my aching head and sticky face. When I had washed, and rinsed my mouth, I felt rather better. Then I took off most of my underclothes and climbed into the bed. With my headache nagging me and my mind running on my predicament, I was afraid of lying awake for the rest of the night. But I didn't; sleep came quickly, and when I woke, it was to hear the door-lock rattling. The Baroness herself carried in a breakfast tray.

'I do not intend to continue to wait on you,' she said. 'You will get up and dress and I shall take you to the salon. There are hardly any servants here. For all meals, we shall serve ourselves.'

With this, she told me more than she realised. I guessed that to the outside world the Palace was to appear empty—of the family, that is—with only a skeleton staff of servants: just the two footmen, a housemaid and a cook, I supposed. And the servants were to remain under the impression that it was Adèle who had returned the night before.

Although I still felt very shaky, my headache had practically gone. I drank the coffee and ate the rolls, which helped. It was now ten o'clock—I had remembered to wind my watch—and it was eleven when the Baroness returned. By then my morale was much better, I had not only washed and dressed, I had used Adèle's brush and comb to do my hair, and felt I could put on a good front to face my captors.

I considered making a bolt for it when the Baroness came, but knew my chances of escape were nil; if I reached the hall and got down the stairs, the wicket would certainly be locked. This idea receded when I saw that the Baroness was not alone. Szarvas was outside the door, and they ranged themselves on either side of me and escorted me to the small salon. There he bowed to me with exaggerated courtesy.

'Pray consider yourself our guest,' he said sarcastically.

I did not bother to answer.

On the earlier occasion I had been in this room, the curtains had been drawn; now they were open, and although I was not allowed to sit near a window, I could see that the main one gave on to a glazed balcony, which had to be the one running round the corner of the building and overlooking the two roads. Time dragged; hardly a word was spoken. For a while, Szarvas and his mother played cards. The house was very quiet; it gave me quite a start when someone began banging on the main door. Although it was distant from where we sat, we could distinctly hear the repeated thuds. I looked up sharply. Szarvas caught me by the wrists.

'No running out on to the balcony and screaming,' he said.

'Yes, it's probably a friend of hers,' his mother remarked. 'He'll soon get tired of knocking at an empty house.'

The knocking did not persist, and after it stopped, the house was silent again except for the sound of passing carriages which reached us faintly from the street below.

When it was time for luncheon, a table was laid in the salon outside the one where we sat, and food placed on the sideboard. Szarvas locked the outer

door as the footman left, and the Baroness indicated I could now go through. We helped ourselves
from the dishes.

It was not a sociable meal. The Baroness and her
son did not speak to me; they hardly spoke to each
other. The feeling grew on me that they were
waiting for something to happen or someone to
come. They were certainly not at ease: perhaps the
thought of being kidnappers did not entirely appeal
to them.

We returned to the little salon, and time passed
even more slowly than before. I had temporarily
stopped being anxious, for it was plain they were
not going to do anything to me of their own accord.

Late in the afternoon, we heard footsteps outside
the room. Whoever it was, they had not banged on
the main door, but must have been expected,
perhaps admitted by a side entrance. Szarvas unlocked the salon door.

With a flurry of silks, Countess Plesch came in,
followed by Palkany, boots and spurs clacking and
jingling. It was uncanny the way the atmosphere
altered at once. Before a word had been spoken,
I was aware of a surge of nervous tension, of
something important being expected, or even
feared.

The quartet greeted each other, and sat down in
a group, Palkany throwing himself casually on to
the sofa beside me, leaning back and studying me
with cool insolence.

'So the Englishwoman has changed places with
Adèle,' he said slowly. 'Well, it need make no
difference.'

'But, Miklas, it must!' the Baroness protested.

'How can we . . . '? Besides, Adèle and Erich are not married! The money . . .'

'Stop fussing about the money, Elsa,' he retorted. 'You can still get her to marry him when everything's over. A delay won't make any difference to that.'

What was he talking about? The others seemed to know.

'No,' he went on. 'All it means is that we shall have to use the Englishwoman instead.'

I resented being spoken about as if I were a horse.

'May I know in what way you intend to use me?' I asked. 'I may not choose to co-operate.'

He smiled at me. It was the most unpleasant smile I had ever seen.

'You may not—yet. As for co-operation, I assure you that you will have no option.'

Countess Plesch seemed quite content to sit and listen; perhaps he had already discussed the matter with her. Szarvas looked merely curious, but the Baroness still raised objections.

'Miklas, I don't see how we can! It's so awkward, keeping her here, and . . .'

'Elsa, leave the thinking to me. I have worked it out. We shall advance our date, that's all. We'll make it tomorrow.'

'*Tomorrow?*'

'Why not? If we wait another week, and Adèle tells what she knows, some action might be taken. If we strike tomorrow, it will be too soon for anyone to have decided anything. If we use *her*'
—he nodded at me— 'and if Adèle starts talking afterwards, well, she's mad, isn't she? She's been in

an asylum—Dietrich can vouch for her obsessions. And we shall be in far too strong a position for anyone to make investigations on the word of a crazy girl.'

'I see,' said the Baroness slowly. 'Yes, I suppose it would work.'

I had a dreadful sinking feeling in my stomach. Fear of the unknown was gnawing at me. Whatever they are planning to involve me in, it was something evil, and it was evil on a large scale. But I could not make even the wildest guess as to what it might be. However, I had the uncomfortable certainty that when Palkany said I would have no option, he knew what he was talking about.

He leaned back and stretched his legs out before him. 'So, our arrangements are as before. I can't stay long now, but I'm free tomorrow. I'll come over during the morning. Tomorrow afternoon we'll do it. Then we'll start afresh, everything will be changed.' There was a gleam in his eyes that was almost fanatical.

'Yes,' Szarvas agreed. 'That's what we need—a new start.'

At last Countess Plesch spoke. 'Then, Erich, you must find Adèle as soon as you can. Get the wretched girl to marry you—you need the money . . .'

'Don't I know it?' he replied. 'My gambling debts alone!'

'Don't talk about trivialities,' said Palkany. 'Or if you must, do it outside. You'd better go and say goodbye—you won't see each other again until the fuss has died down.'

'That's true,' said Countess Plesch with a sigh.

So, whatever was happening tomorrow, she was not actively involved.

'*Himmel!* How I wish that damned husband of mine would die!'

The sudden viciousness of the remark, and the expression on her face which had changed from near-boredom to cold hatred, both sickened and frightened me. That charming, kind old man . . .

'Don't be silly, my dear,' Palkany reproved her. 'You should be grateful for him. He's the best protection you could have.'

She shrugged, and going over to the Baroness, bade her goodbye. 'We shall meet later,' she said. 'Come, Erich, see me out.'

Szarvas left the room with her, putting one arm about her waist.

'I'll give them a few minutes for their tender farewells,' said Palkany.

The Baroness looked at him appealingly. 'We'll be together, won't we, Miklas?'

'I expect so—most of the time.'

She gave him a doubtful glance, and he got up, went over and sat beside her. As though they were alone in the room, she threw herself into his arms, clung around his neck and kissed him.

'My dear . . .' he began.

'I'm nervous, Miklas. It will be all right, won't it?'

'Of course it will! By tomorrow evening, we won't have a care in the world.'

It quite disgusted me, the way she clung to him and kissed him. He seemed to tolerate it, no more, and it was her utter slavishness and adoration that revolted me, not her passion. I turned my head away, thinking, could I kiss Piers like that? Yes, why not? But only if he felt the same about me. How wonderful that would be! He had once loved someone like that; when he explained to me about a young man's love, he *knew*. He had got over that, but I could not hope to be his second love. To him, I'm just a headstrong young girl. At this very minute he's probably cursing me for disappearing and causing him a lot more trouble. Was it Piers who had knocked at the door? Would he manage to find me? Within me, fear and apprehension grew. Palkany had some evil plot arranged, I was to be forced into it, and it was growing less and less likely that Piers or anyone else would intervene in time.

Palkany was disentangling himself from the Baroness's embrace and bidding her goodbye.

Time dragged on. We had tea; we had supper; and as soon as we left the table, Szarvas and the Baroness took me back to Adèle's room. I was locked in for the night.

There were books on the shelves, and I tried to read—anything to stop my mind from speculating on what the next day would bring. I had run out of ideas as to what Piers might be doing, and tomorrow's events would seem to be more important. But I could not concentrate; my mind kept turning over what had been said that afternoon, trying to find a clue, coming up with nothing.

I have never known time to drag as it did all through that day. It was a day I shall never forget, and I shall always remember the date—Tuesday the twenty-ninth of January 1889—the longest day in my life.

I went to bed. For hours, it seemed, I tossed and turned, but eventually I fell into a fitful sleep. Had I known what Wednesday would bring, I would not have slept a wink.

The next morning, the routine of my imprisonment took the same course. The Baroness and her son were in a state of suppressed excitement, but while he was jaunty, she seemed nervous, almost fearful. When Palkany appeared, she threw herself into his arms and said in a strangled whisper,

'Are you going to do it?'

He did not even pretend to be tolerant of her nervousness. 'Elsa, don't be ridiculous! Do you think I've been working so long for this to give it up now? It's the only way, I tell you.'

He unclasped her arms, saw her seated on the sofa and took his place beside her.

'But—should it be *now*?'

'I have told you, now is the right time! Rudolf has come out for us! What better sign could we want? Five days ago, Karolyi—one of Rudolf's best friends—disputing the Army Bill in Parliament! He would never have dared to attack the German-language examination for Hungarian officers without Rudolf's approval! Rudolf is for an independent Hungary—and is ready to support us! It couldn't be clearer!'

This was the first inkling I had received that Palkany's plot was political. For a few moments it floored me completely. Political action—some sort of support for Hungary being independent of the Empire—a total upheaval in Franz Josef's unification of so many nationalities under one rule, an upheaval which would be supported by the Crown

Prince. Even I, ignorant as I was in matters political, could see that it would be a very serious matter. But, in such a plot, how could Adèle, or myself, possibly fit in? How would I be 'used'?

'Have you told the servants we are leaving today?' Palkany asked the Baroness.

'Yes. I've done all you said. The carriage is ordered.'

'Good. We can have luncheon, and then prepare for action. Not that there's much to do.'

He glanced across at me.

'Our English friend is looking puzzled—as well she might. I think the time has come to tell her what she is going to do.'

The Baroness started to protest, but he ignored her. He told Szarvas to check that the balcony windows were shut, and then to close those leading to it from the room. He smiled at me.

'We can't have you making a commotion that might be heard outside. Erich, sit beside her, and at the least move, control her. I warn you, Lady Charlotte! Make the slightest protest at any time from now on, and you will be bound and gagged.'

I thought of asking what use I could possibly be in that state, but Palkany was looking at me with that daunting glitter in his eyes, and I kept silent.

'What we are going to do, Lady Charlotte, is quite simple and will be most effective. We are going to assassinate the Emperor.'

He might have been talking of drowning a cat! He showed no emotion, no compunction whatever. I sat and stared at him, and silence seemed to fill the room like a palpable thing.

'You are surprised? It may appear drastic to you,

but it is the only way. A sudden blow—Rudolf acceding to the throne—a ruler sympathetic to our cause. He will give us independence. One man's life, against thousands that might be lost in a revolution that might not even succeed.'

'Your arrogance amazes me!' I said, when I could find words. 'You're playing God with one man's life—or thousands . . .'

'I am doing what must be done for my country!' His eyes blazed with a cold fire. 'Do not dare to criticise me!'

Then he damped down his anger and turned to baiting me. 'But surely you want to know how you will be concerned?'

'I imagine you are about to tell me.'

'You may as well know. It will give you something to look forward to.'

He had brought a leather pouch into the room with him, and now he picked it up from where he had placed it beside the sofa. The Baroness was looking at him as if mesmerised. He opened the pouch and drew out two rounded metal objects, each about the size and shape of a small pineapple.

'Do you know what these are?' he said to me.

'I am not sure.'

'They are grenades—a kind of bomb, you would say. One to use, and one as a reserve.'

He put them back, and set the pouch down on the floor again.

'And this is what will happen. During the afternoon, the Emperor will drive past here on his way to an official engagement. As you know, the balcony is perfectly situated to give us a view of his approach. When his carriage is almost underneath us, I shall light the fuse and drop the grenade. The rule of Franz Josef will be ended.'

I could not answer. No one else spoke. Szarvas was watching me, the Baroness had turned very pale and was sitting hunched up, hands clasped, in the corner of the other sofa.

Palkany went on, 'And now we come to your part in the affair. I could not trust you to throw the grenade—women have such poor aim!—but you are nevertheless going to play the assassin. Directly after the explosion I shall blow your brains out, with a lady's dainty little pistol which will be left in your hand. Szarvas and I will join Elsa in the carriage, and we shall leave through a back exit quite unobtrusively amid the hubbub. The house will be empty, as the servants have been given the afternoon off. When they return, they will find that we have left, after luncheon, as planned; but that an Englishwoman with a grudge against the Emperor must have crept into the house as we left, and having achieved her object, blew her brains out. She lies on the floor of the balcony, an open window above her and a spare grenade at her side. By that time, we shall be on the road to my estate in Hungary.'

I sat and took it all in. The plot was childish, but it could succeed. Whether it did was not likely to concern me. Then another thought struck me, and I looked across at the Baroness, sitting pale-faced but in control of herself.

'And you were going to do this—with *Adèle*?'

She did not answer, but I saw guilt in her eyes.

'But you wanted her to marry your son first —otherwise getting the money might be more complicated, if she were considered a murderess as well as a suicide?'

Palkany nodded. 'You have quite a quick brain, my dear. Yes. Poor Adèle, of course, would have committed the act in one of her unbalanced moments. Still, you have made one little matter easier for us. Erich can take his time about marrying her now.'

'I think you're all mad!' I cried. 'What do you expect to get out of this ghastly business?'

'We each have our own aims,' Palkany said suavely. 'Hungarian independence—a high position in the state or the army—money, naturally . . .'

'And you?' I said to Baroness Elsa. 'What will you get?'

'What I want,' she replied.

I was not so sure.

What did it matter? What did any of it matter to me? What concerned me was that I was to die so that they could be free of the consequences of their action, unsuspected, unpunished. I could not see any way of avoiding the fate they had prepared for me. It was so simple for them. All they had to do was to keep me quiet until the murder was done. Afterwards, the servants would assume that Adèle had left with the Baroness, and that I, who knew the house well enough to find my way to the balcony, had got inside when the door was unlocked.

I'll wait until I hear a servant in the next room, I thought, and then I'll scream—shout 'Murder!' or 'Help me!'—there's nothing else I can do.

But they had thought of that. Before the servant

came up to lay the table for luncheon, my hands had been tied and my mouth gagged.

'It will save us explaining that Adèle has had a raving fit,' Palkany said ironically.

I was released for luncheon.

I was feeling sick with horror, tenseness knotting my stomach, my mouth dry and my chest contracted. But, whatever happened, I was not going to show these people that I was afraid. I sat down at the table, drank some wine, let it moisten my mouth and throat and ease my tension and sickness, and began to eat. Silently and steadily I plodded through the meal. Food inside me must help my courage, I thought, and remembered the traditional breakfast for a man about to hang. Palkany eyed me, I thought, with a certain critical admiration.

'Do you think we won't do it?' he said at last.

'I think you will, if you can,' I answered. 'And I cannot prevent it.'

'I'm sorry we can't provide you with a priest,' he said with heavy sarcasm.

'Do not worry. I am not very religious.'

In fact I was wishing that religion meant more to me; it might have given me some comfort.

We went back to the little salon, and waited. The Baroness was getting more nervous, and kept looking at the clock.

Finally Palkany snapped, 'Elsa, pull yourself together! There's an hour to go yet!'

'This waiting is dreadful for the nerves! May I go out on to the balcony?'

'I suppose so. But keep behind the shutters.'

She opened the window and went through. Some

of the balcony shutters were closed; she stood behind one and looked sideways down into the street. Her gaze, at first idle, became intent, and she stayed there for two or three minutes. When she came in, she seemed more agitated.

'Miklas, there's something going on,' she said. 'It's very quiet, and the people—they seem to be gathering in little groups, talking and then moving on, as if something unusual had happened.'

'You're imagining it,' he retorted, but went out to the balcony to see for himself.

'You're right,' he said grudgingly when he came back. 'But it could be anything—a train accident, or one of the opera stars suddenly taken ill— nothing to concern us. They're just spreading a bit of gossip.'

It was true, the street had become quiet. The *Fasching* noises of people enjoying themselves in a variety of crazy ways at all hours of the day and night had stopped. It was uncanny. Szarvas looked out for a moment.

'Something has dampened *Fasching*,' he said. 'Even that drunken devil has gone home.'

'What drunken devil?' asked the Baroness, as if she must say something or scream.

'Oh, a fellow in a devil suit. He was outside this morning—collapsed against the lamp-post opposite—dead drunk. I imagine he came round and found it a bit cold for him.'

A devil suit! My heart leapt—oh, please, let it be Piers! I prayed. And then common sense returned. There must be dozens of men with devil suits in Vienna, and if it had been Piers, he would have seen no signs of life, and he had no reason to believe I was in the Palace. He had gone—where? Back to the Embassy—anywhere . . . He was not going to be able to do anything for me. And time was passing, slowly, oh, so slowly, but inexorably.

We heard the servants leave the house, passing under the balcony and on down the street. Then Palkany signed to Szarvas. He seized my wrists, and as I opened my mouth to scream, Palkany thrust a gag between my jaws. Quickly and efficiently they bound me hand and foot, and dumped me back on the sofa.

'Ten minutes to go,' said Palkany to the Baroness. 'You can go down to the carriage, Elsa.'

With a sigh of relief, she got up, and avoiding my eyes, hurried out of the room. And that's the last I shall see of her, I thought, and felt cold with dread.

The two men went out to the balcony, keeping hidden behind the shutters. Through the open window I could hear everything they said.

'Something is going on, Miklas,' Szarvas insisted. 'People are behaving strangely.'

'It's nothing that concerns us.'

I sat there, watching the clock, with the appalling knowledge of what the men were about to do, and the ghastly sensation that my own time was running out as well. At least, this would be the worst part, I thought—the waiting. When death came, it would be sudden, over in an instant. The men, I could see, were getting tense.

Szarvas pulled out his watch. 'We should hear it any moment now,' he said.

Amid the subdued street noises came the distant sound of more carriage-wheels, and Palkany's hand went into his pouch. The carriage came nearer.

'It's not him!' said Szarvas. 'That's not a royal carriage!'

'Are you sure?'

'Certain.'

'But he's due—any second . . .'

'It's not him!'

'*It must be!*'

'*No!*'

The carriage rattled past.

'He's late,' said Szarvas.

'He's never late!' hissed Palkany. 'With him, everything goes to the minute—the second. He lives like clockwork!'

'I know! But I tell you he's late! Trouble with the horses—something simple . . .'

'It's all provided for!' said Palkany. 'He's *never* late!'

They stood there waiting, listening, as if stupefied, and still the Emperor's carriage did not come. Suddenly Palkany began to laugh.

'Would you believe it, Erich!' he gasped. 'I believe Fate has stepped in for us! The Emperor's ill! There's nothing else that could make him late! That's what the folk are gossiping about! *He's seriously ill!* Cheer up! Perhaps he died in the night—a heart attack, perhaps—the news wouldn't be released at once. They'd lead up to it by saying he was ill . . .'

'Of course!' Szarvas answered, and I could hear the relief in his voice. 'After all, he's fifty-eight —works himself hard—hasn't been looking too well—he *must* be ill!'

'But we can't be sure,' retorted Palkany swiftly. 'It may be some trivial thing. I'll stay here, ready to do what's necessary if he does come. You go and see what you can find out. Come back as soon as you can. Don't go far. If he comes, I'll do it, and you'll hear it and can run back and join us. But I won't wait for you. If you can't join us, you'll still be in the clear.'

'Yes. Very well.'

Szarvas hurried out.

As for me, gagged and trussed up like a chicken, I was left alone with Palkany.

CHAPTER ELEVEN

PALKANY WAS plainly furious at the delay, at the hitch in his plans. And he was getting nervous, too. I could guess what he was thinking. If the Emperor doesn't come, can we wait another day? What is going on out there?

He did not leave the balcony. He did not dare, in case the Emperor's carriage came. He paced up and down behind the shutters, and gave me some venomous glances as if I were responsible for this inexplicable lateness. I had the feeling that if he had come into the room, I should have suffered. With him, gallantry did not go below the surface; he was no respecter of women. I could hear him muttering to himself, but I could not understand a word. Probably he was cursing in his native Hungarian —it certainly sounded like it. Minutes dragged on, and the deathly quiet outside seemed to invade the room. It was as though everything had ground to a halt, was in a state of suspended animation. Was the whole of Vienna stilled into this kind of catalepsy?

Then we heard running feet coming through the large salons. Szarvas burst into the room, with the Baroness panting behind him. Both were very pale.

Palkany strode towards them. 'What is it?'

At first Szarvas could not speak clearly. Incoherently, he began, 'It's not the Emperor—no one seems to know—dozens of rumours—it's bad . . .'

The Baroness began to cry.

'Pull yourself together, Erich!' Palkany snapped. *'What have you heard?'*

'Rumours—about *Rudolf*—an accident—but no one knows anything definite. I stopped a messenger-boy—he was wearing a black armband—but *he* didn't know what for! But there's something very wrong. Everything's cancelled for tonight—the opera—plays—cabarets—balls—the whole of *Fasching*—and though no one knows anything for certain, they think it's Rudolf . . .'

Palkany stood rigid, the colour visibly receding from his face, his eyes gaining brilliance so that they burned in their sockets. His mouth worked.

'What shall we do?' Szarvas asked.

The Baroness began to moan. Palkany turned on her savagely.

'Shut up, Elsa! Stop snivelling and let me think!' They waited.

'If there is some trouble with Rudolf, we can't risk anything. We must wait and see how bad it is.'

'There's even a rumour that he's dead!'

'It's not *possible*! And yet he was going to the hunting-lodge on Monday—there could have been an accident . . .'

'What shall we do?'

Palkany came to a decision. 'We must leave. We'll make for the lodge at Marienwald. I've papers there that must not fall into the wrong hands. By the time we arrive, we'll have found out the truth of things. When we know, we can decide whether it's safe to come back to Vienna, or whether to go on to

Hungary. You'd better stay here, Elsa, and see if you can find Adèle.'

The Baroness burst into a torrent of tears and sobs.

'I'm not leaving you, Miklas! How shall I know what's happening? All our plans . . .'

He gave her a long, calculating look. 'Like all women, I doubt if you can keep your mouth shut. With what you know, you'll be safer with me. You can come.'

Szarvas gestured to me.

'What about her?'

'Damn her! She's bad luck!' Palkany said viciously.

'She knows too much!' cried the Baroness. 'Shoot her now!'

She's as bad as they are, I thought, in a different way.

'*Now?*' retorted Palkany. 'Use your head! Leave her here, shot? We'd be dragged into the enquiry! You're right that she knows too much—so we'll take her with us.'

'Take her with us?' the Baroness repeated incredulously.

'She's nothing but a nuisance!' said Szarvas.

'She's a dangerous nuisance. Oh, I'm not suggesting saddling ourselves with her for long. But we'll take her part of the way. We're going to Marienwald. Don't you think it would be *suitable* if she committed suicide near her father's grave? A grief-stricken daughter? I don't think many questions would be asked.'

'Yes! That's a brilliant idea, Miklas!' With Palkany again in control and directing them on new lines, Szarvas's confidence had returned and he was ready for action again. 'Are we going now?'

'We've nothing to stop for. Elsa, get a cloak for her.'

'Why should I? Let her get cold—she'll be dead soon, anyway.'

'*Get a cloak!* We may want to cover her, you fool!'

The Baroness drew in her breath sharply, and her petulant mouth tightened. Then, gathering her own cloak about her, she flounced out of the room. Next the men left me, but it was only for a few moments, to collect their great-coats. The Baroness came back with one of Adèle's cloaks. Szarvas untied my feet, Palkany threw the cloak about me, and between them they forced me across the salons, down the stairs, and into the courtyard where a carriage was waiting, the horses moving restlessly.

'You drive first, Erich,' said Palkany. 'And see what you can find out on the way.'

The Baroness got in, and I was pushed in after her. When I nearly fell, no one attempted to save me. Palkany thrust me into a seat, held the horses while Szarvas mounted the box and took the reins, saw the carriage through a back exit into a mews, and closed the courtyard doors. Then he joined us inside, and we passed out of the mews into the street. We were on our way out of Vienna.

First we had to drive through part of the old town. Several times Szarvas stopped and asked for news, but although everyone seemed stunned and silent, nobody was certain of anything. But they all agreed that something terrible had happened, and that Prince Rudolf was at the centre of it. It was as if the mere threat of tragedy involving the Crown Prince had paralysed everything.

'We're going on,' said Palkany. 'On to Marienwald. I want those papers.'

I did not understand what was concerning him. Papers he had considered safe yesterday might not be safe tomorrow—it was odd reasoning. But I had nothing to do with it. What concerned me was that, although I had been given a reprieve, the nearer we got to Marienwald the closer I was to death.

The winter dusk had drawn in, though it was still afternoon, and it was cold in the carriage. The Baroness began complaining, pulling at her fur-lined cloak more tightly and sitting closer to Palkany.

'Why couldn't we have stayed?' she whined. 'We could have got the servants back and been comfortable there—we haven't *done* anything! Or we could have gone to the Feldbach house—for all we know, Adèle has gone there . . .'

'Elsa!' he exclaimed irritably. 'Adèle's one of the reasons why we couldn't stay! With none of us around, she'll probably tell all she knows—and though we're not sure how much it is, it will be enough to make things damned awkward if Rudolf's ill and can't protect us. I wish you'd use your head.'

'Miklas, I'm not clever like you! But I *have* helped. I wish you'd be a little bit grateful to me.'

'You helped because you wanted Adèle's money,' he said caustically. 'Now you haven't got it, and you're not likely to. You were going to help me with some of it, remember?'

'I'm still not a poor woman.'

'No—you're a moderately rich one, with expensive tastes.'

She sulked for a little while. Then, 'Miklas, I'm getting hungry. What are we going to do about food?'

Since we were now jolting along a country road in virtual darkness, I saw little prospect of nourishment. I don't suppose they'll bother to feed me, I thought. But if only they'd take this gag out! My mouth is so dry, and stretched at the corners, it will never go back into place again. As if that matters now!

Palkany might have read my thoughts. He leaned over and untied the gag. 'You can shout your head off now, no one will hear you.'

I was grateful; it was the first sign of consideration I'd had from him.

'Will you release my wrists?' I asked.

'No.'

So that was that; but I was not so uncomfortable now.

'What about food, Miklas?'

'We'll stop at an inn and get something.'

After a while, the men decided to change places. This might be my opportunity, I thought. Palkany got out; Szarvas was standing by the horses; I stood up and took a flying jump out of the door. I had to jump sideways, and with my hands tied it was difficult to balance. I stumbled and fell. Even without the fall, I do not think I could have got away.

As it was, Palkany turned, swift as a snake, and seized me, dragging me to my feet and shaking me viciously. 'You little devil!' he said between his teeth. 'Get back inside!' He pushed me up the step and back into the carriage.

'Elsa, can't you do a damn thing?' He turned back to me. 'Try that again, and I'll tie your legs and gag you for good!'

I was lucky to get away so lightly. I think he had more important things than me on his mind.

Our progress was slow, necessarily so, on a dark icy country road with only the carriage lights to show us the way. Szarvas and his mother exchanged hardly a word. Once she said to him, 'What are we going to do, Erich?' and he replied, 'Leave it to Miklas. When we find out what has happened, he'll know what is best.'

After what seemed a very long time, Palkany drew the horses to a halt. Szarvas let down the window and stuck his head out.

'Do you want me to take over?'

'No. Gag the girl and tie her feet. I think we're coming to a place where we might get some food.'

Szarvas did what he was told.

'It's done.'

'Right. I think there's an inn just over this rise. When we get there, you, Elsa, go inside and get some food packed up for us—whatever they've got ready—bread, meat, cheese, and a couple of bottles of wine. We'll eat on the way.'

'Oh, Miklas, can't we stop?'

'You can have something there while they're preparing it, if you must. I'll stay up here, and you, Erich, sit the girl in the corner and cover her so that it looks as if she's asleep.'

'Understood.'

'Miklas, can't we stop for the night?' the Baroness pleaded.

'No, we can't. We need the time. One can drive while the other sleeps. Besides, what would we do about *her*?'

'Damn her! The sooner we get rid of her the better! Why not now?'

Palkany did not answer, but drove on. To everyone's relief he was right; there was an inn just over the rise, which opened to the Baroness's knocking, and she went inside. It's probably the first time she's had to do anything for herself, I thought—but as far as her own comfort was concerned, she was not a fool. We waited for some time, and when she came out, accompanied by a boy carrying a bundle and a couple of bottles of wine, she looked better tempered and there was colour in her cheeks. She had eaten, and warmed herself by the inn fire. As she took her seat beside me, the waft of her breath told me that she had given herself some inner warmth with a glass of brandy punch.

Szarvas suggested a change of places with Palkany, who must be cold from driving.

'No. You eat first, then we'll change.'

Szarvas got out the food as we swayed and jolted on. It was exactly what Palkany had predicted —bread, meat and cheese. The meat was slices of beef and tongue and sausage. I longed for some—I decided that fear accentuated hunger in me—but was not offered any.

'Give me some, Erich,' said the Baroness petulantly. 'I had only a bite inside.'

She ate and drank—from the cup of a hip-flask Szarvas produced—he drank from the bottle.

When they had finished, he shouted to Palkany, and they changed places. The journey recommenced, and Palkany ate. Then he turned to me.

'Do you want something?'

I nodded.

'Let her starve!' said the Baroness maliciously, but he took out the gag and untied my hands.

He gave me wine, too, handing me the remains of a bottle with the warning, 'Don't do anything silly!'

By then I was too tired and dispirited to think of hitting anyone with it. It wouldn't have helped me.

When I had finished, he retied my hands but released my feet. He was being kind to me to irritate the Baroness, I thought, and knew I was right when he removed the rope and ran his hands over the top of my boots, saying, 'Quite a neat pair of ankles.'

I thought of kicking him but didn't—it would only provoke him further.

The Baroness rose to the bait. 'There's no need for that, Miklas!'

'No need, my dear! But I'll snatch at anything to brighten this dull journey.'

'Can't you ever leave women alone?' she snapped.

'You would not care for it if I did.'

'You know perfectly well I mean *other* women!'

'Don't be boring, Elsa. One does what appeals to one at the time—that's a man's prerogative.'

Now she stopped being angry and started pleading. 'Oh, you won't! Miklas, you *won't*! You said you loved me best of all. After we're married, you'll give up the others, won't you?'

'After we're married! My dear, you're looking a long way ahead.'

He sat there smiling, goading her.

'You said you'd marry me . . . *When*, Miklas?'

'I don't remember saying so. Talk of marriage has been all on your side, my dear. How can we make plans at present? Just now, we have to wait and see what tomorrow brings.'

This seemed to turn his mind from baiting her to thinking about the situation facing him.

'Why don't you go to sleep? Erich and I will have to take it in turns.'

The night wore on. From what passed between the two men as they changed places, I discovered that they were skirting Baden and going by a difficult country route to join the Marienwald road some miles out of the city. And this turned out to be a blessing for me, because they reached a point where in the dark they could not be sure of the road; and, in addition, the horses were tiring. They decided to stop for an hour or two, and resume the journey when the false dawn showed a few landmarks.

I tried to sleep as well, and I think I dozed, but I was beset by nightmares between sleeping and waking, so I hardly knew what was real and what was conjured up by my overwrought nerves.

When we restarted, the Baroness was in a worse temper than before. Palkany was with us again.

'When are you going to get rid of her?' she asked.

'Quite soon. Outside Marienwald.'

'What with?'

'The pistol, of course. An English lady is hardly likely to provide herself with a grenade in normal circumstances. But she could well have a pistol for her protection,' he explained, as though to a silly child.

'That's what I thought. Let me see it, Miklas.'

'Why?'

'Because—well, I want *her* to see it. I want her to know we mean business.''

'I think Lady Charlotte knows that by now,' he said smoothly. 'Still, here it is.'

From an inside pocket he drew out a small pistol and held it out on the palm of his hand. It was only about five inches long, with a short squat barrel and an ivory handle. Although it looked like a toy, the barrel was fat, and I knew it would take a bullet the size of which would certainly kill at close quarters. I felt a shudder down my spine and my back muscles contracted.

She took it from him, turned it over in her hand, and held it under my nose.

'You see?' she said.

If I had ever thought her pretty, I did not then. The blue eyes were cold as ice, the soft mouth vicious.

'Is it ready to fire, Miklas?'

'No.'

She handed it back to him.

'The sooner the better!' she said.

I looked out of the window. The sun was rising, but hardly visible through cloud and haze. The winter landscape looked colder, more cheerless, than ever. Thick snow on the mountains; thin snow on the distant fields; I could hear the wheels churning through ice and slush on the road. I remember thinking, They'll have to find a place without snow, to avoid leaving tracks . . .

We were near Marienwald now. The land was deserted, no one working in the countryside, no one abroad on the road. Who would go out from choice on a raw winter morning? Then I was surprised to hear for the first time the sound of hooves. A horseman was coming up behind us, but our carriage-wheels had drowned the thud of his approach until he was quite near.

Szarvas, who was now inside with us, put his head out of the window and looked back. Then he called to Palkany.

'It's all right. He looks like some kind of mail-carrier. He's got big leather pouches.'

Desperation raised the foolish hope in me—could it be Piers in disguise, riding up alone to rescue me? Palkany reined in the horses, and the man came alongside. I could see him only from shoulder to waist as he passed the window, and still in my folly I hoped. But he came along quickly and would have overtaken us, had not Palkany called to him. They exchanged words; their voices were muffled; after a few moments the man rode on. Considering the state of the road, he was pressing his horse hard and fast. To my surprise, Palkany did not drive on. Instead I heard him get off the box, and the next moment he appeared at the window and stared in. His face was pale, eyes burning, mouth and jaw tense. He was holding a newspaper.

'The morning paper—on the train from Baden,' he said, and pushed it through the window.

Szarvas took it. There was no need to open it; one glance at the front page told everything. The *Wiener Tagblatt* for Thursday the thirty-first of

January—the whole of it below the heading edged with a thick black border, bearing at the top three words, and three exclamation marks:

UNSER KRONPRINZ TOT!!!
OUR CROWN PRINCE DEAD!!!

In the silence, the Baroness gave an anguished gasp. For several seconds no one spoke. Then,

'*Dead?*' Szarvas said incredulously.

'*Dead?* Of what?' the Baroness asked.

'A stroke—they say . . .' Szarvas told her as he scanned the page. 'I can't believe it! *Rudolf*—a stroke?'

'What the hell does it matter?' Palkany burst out bitterly. 'It could be anything—it makes no difference. *He's dead!*'

'What do we do?'

A fine officer Szarvas must be, I thought. In every emergency he has to ask for directions.

'What we decided last night,' Palkany told him crisply. 'Get to my hunting-lodge—destroy the papers—get fresh horses and make the best time we can to Hungary.'

'What about her?' pressed the Baroness.

'I'll deal with her on the way.'

I caught a glimpse of Marienwald village on our left. We veered off on a side road to the right. The men had changed places again, but Szarvas obviously knew the way. The Baroness was at last cowed into silence by the seriousness of the situation, and sat in her corner, huddled among her furs, plying her handkerchief at intervals. I was cold and very stiff. I had no feeling in my hands, but my feet, since my ankles were not bound, were not so numb, and they hurt. Numbness seemed to be invading me; I could not think of any way of attempting to save myself. I was like a dumb animal going to the slaughterhouse.

Palkany eyed me up and down. 'I'll say this for you—you're not the whimpering type,' he remarked.

When I did not answer, he went on.

'It will give me great pleasure to deal with you. Your family are bad luck to me. First your father —now you.'

Suspicion crystallised in my mind. 'So my father crossed your path—not just as a hunting guest?'

'A hunting guest? That's a joke! I'll tell you. He saw Adèle once—and that was enough. She told him something she had overheard, which was very silly of her. So we had to deal with him. No, he wasn't a hunting guest—rather, a hunted one.' His laugh was like the snarl of a wolf. 'How would you like to die where he did?'

Now I was not suspicious: I knew. 'You killed him!'

'Yes. He interfered. He made himself a danger to our cause. He signed his own death-warrant. Like father, like daughter. You too interfered, and you too must die. You know too much. It would be quite poetic, for you to die in the same place.'

'And suspicious,' I said.

'Well,' he shrugged, 'we won't make it in the same spot—but the same area—that will do nicely.'

I looked out of the window so that he should not see fear in my eyes and thought, You fiend! It was your hand that killed my father! I should have realised earlier that it was not an accident.

The road had become very narrow, with trees on either side of us, a pine forest. We threaded our way, the road twisting at intervals, always going deeper into the forest. This must be the road leading to his hunting-lodge—and probably nowhere else. We would not meet anyone on the way, except, perhaps, a forester in Palkany's pay, who would conveniently forget having seen us.

'This will do,' Palkany said, and thrusting his head out of the window, called to Szarvas to stop. He got out of the carriage and dragged me after him.

The Baroness got out, too. 'I'm coming,' she said. 'I want to watch this.'

'You can be useful. Erich, stay with the horses —we shan't be long. Now hold her, and see she doesn't run for it,' he said to the Baroness.

When she had a tight grip on me, he let me go. I struggled, but she pinned me against the side of the carriage. Palkany brought out the little pistol, and felt in his pocket again. He opened the pistol and charged it with a fat cartridge.

'Only one?' said the Baroness.

'My dear, it holds only one shot—but one is enough.'

He replaced it in his pocket and grasped my arm. 'This way,' he said.

The three of us plunged into the trees. I admit I dragged my feet: with death so near, I was in no hurry. We were well inside the wood when we reached a clearing, and Palkany stopped.

'This is far enough,' he said. 'Untie her hands and rub them,' he ordered the Baroness. 'If she's found soon, we don't want it to be obvious that she's been tied up.'

He had my forearms in a tight grip. The Baroness was not good at untying knots, and she kept dealing me vicious glances as she struggled with delicate fingers and long nails at the harsh rope. But she managed it.

'Put the rope in my pocket—no, the other one!'

This was my cue to struggle again, and I did so with all my strength, kicking at Palkany's legs as well, but it was no use. He was far too strong for me, and was wearing high boots—I was like a fly in a spider's web.

'Hold her!' said Palkany, and the Baroness caught my wrists. Still gripping me with one hand, he put the other in his pocket and drew out the pistol.

I saw the fat barrel pointing at me—coming nearer—he would put it to my temple, and then —with one explosion it would be the end of Charlotte Brantham. Well, I was my father's daughter. I wouldn't whimper or plead. I saw the wolf-face with the snarling smile—the barrel coming closer still—and then . . .

'*Miklas!*'

The one word, shouted in Szarvas's voice, reached us faintly through the trees. Palkany swung round, head back, and we heard the sound of someone breaking through the undergrowth.

For a full three seconds he waited; then—he saw the man. It was not Szarvas. With a curse he turned back to me, but surprise had momentarily loosened his grip, while the Baroness had let go and clapped her hands to her face in fear. Using all my strength,

I twisted myself out of his own detaining hand, and ran—or rather stumbled—for cover. But my feet were cold, and the ground was littered with stumps and roots, so that I had hardly taken five steps before I fell.

As I crashed down on my side, I could see Palkany raising his hand to aim the pistol at me, while behind him the stranger came towards us. Then there was the sound of a shot, deafening to my ears, and I could not understand why I felt nothing, why Palkany staggered, let the pistol drop from his hand, and fell to the ground within a yard of me. Then I saw that the stranger held a gun, large and black and lethal-looking, and the barrel was veiled in wisps of smoke.

The Baroness, who had been standing as if petrified, rushed forward and flung herself down beside Palkany. She caught him in her arms, lifted him, and I could then see the great red stain welling out from under his half-open great-coat. I was aware of the horror of it, but the relief of being alive myself was so great that for the moment I could do nothing—I could not even get up from the ground.

'Miklas! *Miklas! No!*'

She screamed the words. His head lolled back, jaw dropping, eyes sightless. I knew as well as she did that he was dead.

The stranger, in his plain dark clothes looking the death-bringer he was, still came towards us, and there were other sounds in the woodland now. But the Baroness seemed to hear nothing, to see nothing but the dead man in her arms. She was moaning, tears pouring down her cheeks. Then I saw her hand go out and pick up the little ivory-handled pistol from where it lay among the dead frost-whitened leaves. She did not hesitate. In one movement she brought it up to her own forehead and pulled the trigger.

I looked away, but not quickly enough. I saw her face become a mangled wreck, saw the blonde hair blotched with blood. The sound of the shot mingled with the other noises—the crashing of feet and the snapping of twigs and branches—and suddenly it seemed as if the clearing was full of people. One of them rushed up to me, flung himself on his knees beside me, and dragged me into his arms.

'Oh, God! My darling!'

It was Piers.

I turned my head and smiled at him. 'Just in time,' I whispered.

Then, for the first time in my life, I fainted.

I came round to find someone rubbing my hands so vigorously that it hurt. Piers's face was above me, drawn and anxious.

'Charlotte! Thank God!'

He released my hands and busied himself pouring something from a hip-flask into its silver cup. As he held it to my lips, I saw that we were in a little two-seater carriage, but we were not moving.

I sipped the brandy and felt my stomach begin to glow. 'How did you find me?' I whispered.

'Explanations later,' he said. 'Did they hurt you?'

'Oh, no. I've been drugged, put in a straitjacket, tied hand and foot, bundled about like a load of washing—but they didn't hurt me!'

I managed a grin, but it did not bring one to his face.

'I should never have let you out of my sight! What you did was madness—trying to release Adèle . . .'

'But I succeeded!'

'At what a cost! You nearly died!'

'You were in time . . .'

My voice tailed off; I hadn't the strength to talk much. I saw the concern in his eyes deepen. He turned and called to someone. There must have been a driver waiting for orders, because at once I heard someone clucking to a horse and we began to move. He took my hands in his again.

'My poor darling—you're still so cold . . .'

His overcoat was already round me on top of Adèle's cloak, and now he tucked it even closer. I felt very tired, too tired to talk, his arm was about my shoulders and I wanted it to stay there—it made me feel safer.

'Hold me, Piers,' I whispered.

My head fell against his chest. His arm tightened. I was enveloped by his strength, at last I felt secure. I must have drifted into a kind of coma; I could not be sure whether he really held me so close against him, as if to warm my body with his, and pressed his lips to my cheek, or whether it was part of my dream of safety. I must have been in a kind of stupor. Then, some time later, I was faintly aware of the movement of the carriage rocking me in Piers's arms, and at last we stopped. We were not in the country any more, for the noises were those of the city, and Piers was lifting me out of the little carriage. He carried me up the steps and into a house, and there was a woman's face looking down at me anxiously. I knew her.

'Mitzi . . .' I whispered.

'That's a good sign,' said Piers. 'She recognises you.'

'Bring her upstairs.'

'I'm not ill . . . just tired . . .'

'Please get her to bed, Mitzi. Give her something hot and let her sleep.'

I tried to protest, but it wasn't worth the trouble. Soon I was in bed, with hot bricks in flannel at my feet and sides, being given sips of hot sweet chocolate. Then I drifted off again.

It was the shock of my experiences, of course, but being young and resilient, it didn't last long. I was soon up and about and demanding to be told what had been going on. In Piers's absence, Mitzi told me what she knew.

Adèle was safe; the servants had got her to the British Embassy, and when Piers had arrived, he had taken over. Since I had not followed soon after Adèle, he started a search. But it was some hours before he could convince the police of the need to search the clinic, and by then I had gone. He immediately thought of the Phoenix Palace, but from his observations it seemed to hold only a few servants. He could see no sign of anyone else there, and it was quite impossible to persuade the police to intervene again.

He then thought I might have been taken to Palkany's hunting-lodge, and set off there—ahead of me, as it happened. When he reached Baden, he found the staff at the railway station like a hive of bees buzzing with rumours. At about nine o'clock that morning Count Hoyos, a close friend of the Crown Prince, who had been spending a few days with the Prince at his hunting-lodge of Mayerling, had driven up in a state of great agitation and had ordered the stationmaster to use a special emergency signal and stop the next train—the Trieste Express. It was unheard-of. The express was stopped; Count Hoyos boarded it, to reach Vienna in the quickest possible time, half an hour. Whatever had occurred, it was of the gravest importance.

'So Piers reached Baden to find the city almost paralysed with rumours,' said Mitzi.

Remembering Vienna, I could well understand it.

'I don't know what he did, or how he did it, but somehow eventually he went with the police to Marienwald, and on to Palkany's lodge. You'll have to ask him for details. You weren't there, but apparently the police found something worth while to them. Then, on the way back, they came across the carriage with young Szarvas beside it. He was arrested—I don't know why—and the rest of them rushed into the woods and found you. That's all I can tell you—except that when Piers brought you here he was quite desperate. Under that calm face, he was nearly out of his mind, thinking you might be dying!'

She was exaggerating, of course; that was Mitzi.

Piers came back that evening, and when he entered the drawing-room and found me there with Mitzi and her husband, his eyes lit up and he gave me a wonderful smile.

'Charlotte! I am so glad to find you better!'

'I am quite well again, thank you, Piers.'

'I don't think you can be yet—but I hope you are

well enough to tell me what happened.'

As I told them, Mitzi's eyes grew wider and rounder, and my story was accompanied by gasps of horror and little outraged cries. Schani listened in bewilderment; Piers took it in silence, but his look grew grimmer and grimmer as my tale progressed.

'And so you found me just in time,' I ended.

'By the grace of God.'

'Now I have some questions to ask you!' I continued.

'I can't promise to answer them, but I'll try.'

At this point, Mitzi found some reason to take Schani away and leave us alone.

'What did you do after you arrived at Baden station?' I asked.

'I went to the police. I had the devil of a job with them—had to battle my way to the Chief, and it took time to convince him that he had a case for searching Palkany's lodge. News of the Crown Prince's death had leaked through, and put them at sixes and sevens, but in a way it helped. I reminded him about your father's death; that we at the Embassy had been convinced he had been silenced, but had agreed not to press for a further investigation. They had wanted his probable murderers to feel secure, for they suspected a political connection and wanted to wait for more information to tighten the net. He agreed at last that there was a possible link with that and Prince Rudolf's death, and that action on his part was advisable. He let me go with his men to the lodge, and there they found evidence of a political plot to declare Hungary independent of the Empire and make Rudolf king of Hungary. That was enough for them, but it did my peace of mind no good whatever! It was pure luck that on the way back we came across the carriage and recognised Szarvas. He was at once arrested as one of the conspirators; and when he shouted a warning to Palkany, I knew you could not be far away.'

'I see. And the man who shot Palkany was a policeman?'

'A plain-clothes detective. He has helped Palkany to cheat the firing-squad, but he has my undying gratitude.'

'What a horrible business it all is!' I said. 'Now, what really happened to Prince Rudolf? The first papers said it was a stroke, but Mitzi says there have been all sorts of different reports.'

'Yes. The first editions said a stroke, or a heart attack. Then they got round to an accidental gun-shot wound—but that edition was confiscated at once.'

'Why?'

'Because the government ministers did not know how to handle the truth. They have now got round to it—in part.'

'In part? And that is . . . ?'

'Suicide.'

'*Suicide?* But why did you say, "in part"?'

He did not answer at once, but looked at me very seriously.

'Charlotte, if I tell you, you must promise to keep it to yourself, to treat it in the utmost confidence. It is only by chance that I have found out what the Court is going to all lengths to hide. If the truth spreads through me, and they find out, I shall be utterly discredited and sent back to London in disgrace.'

'I shan't tell a soul, Piers. But why are you trusting me with it?'

'I feel you have a right to know. If it hadn't happened, you would be dead. You are, in a distant way, involved.'

'But why is it being kept so secret? What did happen?'

'The Court cannot face the thought of the scandal which would spread all over Europe. Their Crown Prince, that adored figure, with wife and daughter . . . shooting himself at his hunting-lodge of Mayerling. That would be terrible enough. But he was not alone. It was a suicide pact. Two hours before killing himself, he had shot his companion, Mary Vetsera.'

'*Mary Vetsera!*'

I thought of the young, sophisticated girl I had glimpsed just once—a fashionable, vibrant figure, the new queen of the smart set—dead, when she had all life before her.

He misunderstood my amazement.

'Yes, it's strange. And she wasn't his official mistress—his affair with Mary Vetsera had been kept incredibly secret. It's so odd, because she wasn't a deluded, dazzled innocent. Oh, yes, she was young—younger than you—but she was experienced, and very ambitious. Yet she chose to die with him. It's like so much that is happening here now—inexplicable. Did she think it would give her some kind of immortality? I wonder if we shall ever understand the human mind?'

'Or the human heart,' I said soberly. 'I thought

the Baroness Elsa was a greedy, shallow woman. Yet when she found Palkany was dead, she shot herself rather than live without him.'

'Don't think about that. It's all over.'

His manner became suddenly businesslike. 'Now, Charlotte, I want you to arrange to go back to England as soon as possible.'

'Piers! Why?'

'Surely you don't want to stay, after all you've been through?'

'I don't know. I don't feel I've seen the real Vienna yet.'

I was thinking, You want to get rid of me. I suppose I deserve it! I've been a nuisance, but I love you so much, and I thought you were beginning to love me.

'You've seen one side of Vienna, and that's the side which will be showing for some time. You've had a series of shocks, and you need to recover from them. Go home and rest, and get fit. You can come back another time, when you and Vienna have both recovered.'

'I may not want to come back then.'

'You will. Come back in spring or summer; then you'll be able to drive in the Prater, go to the Vienna woods, drink the new wine in the little country inns, hear the Opera, and dance all night to Strauss music. That's the other Vienna, and you'll love it. But that's for another year.'

I felt empty, forsaken. 'Will you be here then, Piers?'

'I don't know. Perhaps. But there will be dozens of young men, all clamouring to take you out, to drive you here and there and dance with you.'

How could I say, 'I would rather do it with you?'

'And you think I should go home now?'

'I do.'

'Very well. But I must see Adèle first. We are sisters. Perhaps—perhaps she would like to come back with me. I'm sure she needs a change of scene.'

'That's a very good idea.'

When Mitzi and I were alone together, she looked at me expectantly. 'Well?'

'Well, what?'

'Did Piers—did you—oh, Charlotte, I left you together on purpose! Don't tell me you didn't come to an understanding?'

'*Understanding?* What are you talking about? All I understand is that he wants to get rid of me. He insists I return to England as soon as possible.'

Mitzi gasped. 'How can he be such a fool! Why do men lose *all* sense when they are in love?'

'Mitzi, he's not in love with me. Sometimes I amuse him—more often than not I exasperate him.'

'*I* think he is in love with you.'

'Mitzi, you are an incurable romantic.'

'What's wrong with that? Let me think. Perhaps he is afraid he is too old for you—or perhaps that he'll be suspected of fortune-hunting, for I would guess you have more money than he has, and besides, you are alone here, and under age—and he is very correct. You are in love with him, aren't you?'

'Yes. But I dare say I shall get over it.'

I knew I wouldn't.

'Then I shall see what I can do.'

'Oh, no!'

'I shall be very tactful.'

This did not give me any hope. If Piers's mind was made up not to love me, nothing would alter it.

It was a week later, about three o'clock on a raw afternoon, and I was once more boarding the Orient Express, this time to return to England. I felt utterly dispirited, which was wrong of me, for I had such kind travelling companions. Adèle was with me. She had jumped at my invitation; not only was she thankful to get away and let her past experiences fade from her mind, but we had become firm friends, and very happy to be sisters in secret. And the problem of a chaperon had been settled in the nicest possible way: Mitzi and Schani had decided it was time they paid a visit to England. So Adèle and I had one double compartment, and they had another in the same carriage.

The platform at the Westbahnhof was alive with the same purposeful, organised activity that I had seen in Paris on the journey out; the same liveried attendants about their varying duties, the same class of passenger bearing the stamp of wealth and good living, with cab-drivers and porters in attendance. The great gleaming train was absorbing traveller after traveller, while others were ready to board and saying their goodbyes. I felt quite wretched. Piers had said his goodbyes to me the previous night at Lady Bellanger's, but I had been cherishing the secret hope that he might find time to come to the station and see us off. But there was no sign of him.

Our reservations had been checked; I cast one

last glance along the platform, and reluctantly followed Adèle and Mitzi into the carriage.

Adèle, who had gained health and strength surprisingly quickly, was pink-cheeked with pleasure and excitement. 'What a splendid train it is!' she said. 'It is so comfortable!'

We settled ourselves. I reminded myself that Adèle had had little opportunity to enjoy herself for years, and that it was up to me to give her a happy time; no matter how miserable I felt I must not let it show. So I did my best, chatting about the train and the journey, while we watched through the window all the bustle going on outside. In a few minutes' time we should be leaving.

A voice said, 'May I come in?'

My heart leapt—I swung round to see Piers in the doorway.

'Piers!'

He smiled and greeted us.

'So you've come to see us off! That is very kind of you.'

I didn't know what else to say. Was I letting my pleasure in seeing him show too much? In another minute he would be leaving again . . .

'Have you everything you need, or is there anything I can get you?' he asked.

'We have everything.'

I could not ask him to write to me—I had no reason to do so. As far as he was concerned, my business in Vienna was finished.

'*En voiture, messieurs, s'il vous plaît!*'

Doors started to slam, the train was about to leave.

'Oh—you must go! Goodbye, Piers!'

He took my outstretched hand and smiled. 'May I join you both at dinner this evening?' he said.

'*Piers!* You're coming too?'

He laughed. 'So may I dine with you?'

I didn't wait for Adèle to speak. 'Of course!'

By the time the attendant announced that dinner was served, I had talked some sense into myself. It meant nothing, I said; he had been recalled to report to the Foreign Office. Still, it would be pleasant to have him with us for the journey; how Lady Bellanger would approve of our being under his protection! Mitzi and Schani, however worthy, were Austrian; Piers was English.

Adèle and I were curious to find out what sort of people were occupying the remaining compartments—one single, one double—which remained in our carriage. We soon saw the single traveller—a man somewhat older than Piers, good-looking, almost too elegant—a Frenchman, we thought. It was a shock to us when, just as we were ready to leave, the other couple passed our half-open door.

They were Count and Countess Plesch. She rustled past in dark green silk decked with diamonds and emeralds, while her husband tottered carefully after her on his two sticks, and we heard her say, 'My dear, Paris will do you a world of good!'

'Don't let her bother you,' I said gently. 'We shall hardly see them—and tomorrow night we should be in London.'

She relaxed, and a few minutes later we went to the dining-car. Piers was already at a table for four, where we joined him; Mitzi and Schani had a table for two across the gangway. Dinner passed pleasantly, but my enjoyment was spoiled by the knowledge that Piers was not there because of me. I knew our relationship must revert to that of acquaintances; I must try to think of him simply as an Assistant Military Attaché, not as the man who once in an unthinking moment called me 'my darling', who wrapped me in his overcoat and held me, gently but firmly, in a jolting carriage while I was in a state of collapse. So my manner to him became a little more formal than it had been of late. The food and wine were superb, and we rounded off with excellent coffee.

Then Adèle said, 'It has been an exciting day, and I am quite tired. Will you both excuse me? Please stay and finish your coffee and brandy—and don't hurry, Charlotte—you won't disturb me.'

'I shall escort you back,' said Piers.

'No, there's no need—look, Mitzi and Schani are leaving, too.'

So Piers and I were alone together.

He sipped his brandy, giving me a shrewd look, and said, 'Charlotte, you are rather formal tonight. Have I done anything wrong?'

'No,' I said, and then sat silent, trying to pick my words. 'Well,' I went on, 'I admit I felt you were hurrying me back to England. I don't blame you—I have caused a lot of trouble.'

'Charlotte, it's not that at all! I didn't want to tell you then, but I will now. I knew that, if you stayed much longer, the Austrian authorities would decide they wanted your evidence in the case against Szarvas. It would be a most unpleasant experience for you—lots of questioning, appearances in court —everything dragging on. Once you are out of the country, you can send a sworn statement through your lawyer, and they can't bother you for anything more.'

'I see.'

I felt a little comforted. There was a long pause.

'Charlotte, would you object if I called upon your aunt and uncle?'

A tiny seed of hope was planted in my heart.

'Which one?' I asked innocently. 'I have five.'

'Oh? Why—Lady Melbury.'

She and her husband were now my legal guardians, and I was to live with them.

'Aunt Hettie. Why do you want to see her?'

'I have a letter of introduction from Lady Bellanger.'

Better and better! Could Mitzi be right? She was certainly correct that Piers would act formally.

'So you want to make her acquaintance? You'd better go in uniform—she adores to see a man in regimentals—if you want to impress her. Though I can't think why you should . . .'

'Can't you? I must meet her in order to call on you. And there's something I want to ask you —with your guardians' permission.'

'Piers! I do believe you're being a stick again! If you've anything to ask me, ask me now! It can't be anything to do with Aunt Hettie.'

Already my heart was thumping; then he flashed me a look of such intensity that it began to bang away so wildly I thought he would hear it.

'I wish I could ask you now. The waiting is killing me. But even if—well, how can I do it in public? Anyone might overhear—it is a private matter —this isn't the time . . . or the place . . .'

What did that matter? Killing him! It was killing *me*! I hunted in my bag and found the little gold pencil that had been Papa's. I had nothing to write on, but the menu card lay at the end of the table, so I picked it up and gave them to him.

'Then write it, Piers.'

For a moment I thought I had gone too far. He gave me another long look, then took the pencil and card, and wrote.

He passed them back to me. I held my breath —and looked. It was a message of military directness:

'Charlotte, will you marry me?'

I tried to look stern; I didn't smile; I wrote one word in block letters and underlined it. Then I handed him the card.

He glanced at me uncertainly before scanning it, then his face broke into a wonderful smile. For I had written 'YES!'

I took back the pencil and put it away. I folded the card, and tucked that away, too. I have it to this day.

He leaned across the table and grasped my hand. Then, in full public view, he raised it to his lips and whispered, 'Charlotte, I love you very much.'

'Oh, Piers, I thought you never would! And I am ridiculously in love with you!'

'That's not ridiculous—it's very sensible!'

He kissed my hand again, then reluctantly let it go.

'When I take you back to your cabin, I shall claim a real kiss. I can't wait for that until we reach England.'

'Nor can I!' I retorted quite shamelessly.

The waiter came to ask if we wanted more coffee. It brought us down to earth for a moment.

I looked up from our table, and saw Countess Plesch. While her husband's eyes were on his plate, hers were busy over his shoulder giving provocative glances to the Frenchman who was travelling alone. Her lover was in prison, her two closest friends were dead, and she was up to her tricks again. Poor, nice old Count, I thought—and that was all. Whatever she did, it was no longer any concern of mine.

I was already thinking of the moment very soon when I should walk ahead of Piers down the swaying corridor until there was no one else in sight. We should stop, and I would turn into his arms. He would hold me close, very close, and then his lips would take mine in a long, sweet kiss. And that kiss would mark the beginning of a new life for me.

I shall never forget that kiss, and the words Piers said to me, as we embraced long and secretly in a swaying corridor of the Orient Express.

THE END

She had everything a woman could want... except love.

Locked into a loveles[s] marriage, Danica Lindsa[y] tried in vain to rekindle th[e] spark of a lost romance. S[he] turned for solace to Micha[el] Buchanan, a gentle yet stro[ng] man, who showed h[er] friendship.

But even as their sou[ls] became one, she knew s[he] was honour-bound to ob[ey] the sanctity of her marria[ge] to stand by her husban[d's] side while he stood trial f[or] espionage even though [her] heart lay elsewhere.

WITHIN REACH
another powerful novel b[y] Barbara Delinsky, author of Finger Prints.

Available from October 1[9]
Price: £2.95. **W●RLDWI[DE]**